T0352566

JAX' HOUSE

Jax' House

Books for older children by John Kitchen:
Nicola's Ghost
A Spectre in the Stones
The Rainbow Talisman (co-author George Acquah-Hayford)
For younger children:
Kamazu's Big Swing Band

UNION BRIDGE BOOKS
An imprint of Wimbledon Publishing Company Limited (WPC)
First published in the United Kingdom in 2016 by
UNION BRIDGE BOOKS
75–76 Blackfriars Road
London SE1 8HA

www.unionbridgebooks.com

Copyright © John Kitchen

All rights reserved. No part of this publication may be reproduced
in any form or by any means without written permission of the publisher.

The moral rights of the author have been asserted in accordance
with the Copyright, Designs and Patents Act 1988.

All the characters and events described in this novel are imaginary
and any similarity with real people or events is purely coincidental.

A CIP record for this book is available from the British Library.

ISBN 978–1–78308–569–9

This title is also available as an ebook.

Permission for use of the poem "An Eos Hweg" has been granted
by the Cornish Language Sociey.

Jax' House

JOHN KITCHEN

1

It was the weirdest thing that had ever happened to Jack O'Hagan.

They'd just arrived in Tregenwyth, and with the furniture van protesting around the tight corners behind them, they were heading for their new house. And, as they manoeuvred down the narrow street, Jack felt an overpowering sensation.

He'd been in this place before. The rugged contours of the houses on each side of the road, the bleak way they crowded together, blocking the light and warmth, the sombre shadows, the drunken steepness of the hill, they all sent the same feeling through him, and as they threaded their way further towards the harbour, the feeling grew.

When his dad pointed out the house they were moving to, Jack caught his breath. Everything about it was so familiar. The narrow frontage and the way it stretched to the sky, the manner in which it shouldered between the other houses; he recognised the random pattern of windows and the cornice running below the roof. He knew the portico and the steps leading to the front door. It was all so much a part of him and yet, as far as he knew, he'd never set foot in Tregenwyth in his life.

His dad and mum had been here.

They'd made several visits in search of their new house, but he'd always stayed back in Stevenage, lodging with a friend.

He didn't want to move and he'd even made a point of not looking at any of the photos Dad took. He liked Stevenage. He was happy with his mates at school and the facilities of a big town.

Tregenwyth was a backwater, remote from everywhere and hundreds of miles from his friends.

He didn't speak as he dragged himself out of the car, even though his dad and mum pressed him for an opinion.

He followed Dad through the gloom of the passageway and then he stopped. He knew the inside of the house as if he'd lived there.

The door to the left would lead into a dining room and the far end of the passage marked the entrance to what would be a large, rambling kitchen with an exit through to a backyard. The yard cut into a sheer cliff of rock and shale. There was a set of twisting stairs to his right, and he knew that would lead to dark landings and rooms looking as though they'd been chucked out at random with not one at the same level as another. He knew the stairs' ultimate location was a small, gloomy attic under the eaves.

There was a larger room, like a lounge, to his right and in the passage, under the stairs, a door that looked as if it opened onto a cupboard. But he knew it wasn't a cupboard. It marked the descent to a cellar.

"Come on then, Jacky boy. Let's have it. What do you make of the place now you've seen it?" his dad said and he swung around. His dad was standing in the passage, framed by the open door, an excited grin on his face, his green eyes sparkling.

"It's a dump," he said. "It's a rickety, musty rat-hole and I can't think why you and Mum wanted to come here. We had a perfectly good house in Stevenage, with all mod-cons."

His dad was a squat man, square faced, with red hair; Irish through and through and proud of it, and to look at, Jack was his stamp, although Jack was smaller. He was thirteen and hadn't yet reached the turning point of an adolescent growth spurt. He had the smooth, unlined complexion of youth, while his dad's face was lined and weatherworn. Dad's hair was peppered with grey, but Jack knew the genetic map would drag him, kicking and screaming, to look just like his father in thirty years' time.

"It's a bit run down," Dad said. "It hasn't been lived in for a couple of years. That's why it smells musty, but it's nothing that a good airing and lick of paint won't put right."

He came down the corridor and put an arm on Jack's shoulder. "Come on, son. This place has got atmosphere. It's got character."

"Yeah," said Jack, pushing the arm away. "So did Jack the Ripper have character, and a cesspit's got atmosphere, but I haven't got to fall in love with them, have I?"

"What's he on about?" said Mum, pushing through the door. She was grasping two heavy cases and they hung like pendulums from her arms. She put the cases down and stared at Jack.

"He thinks it's a dump," Dad said.

His mum grunted. "Teenage strop. They think they're modern and 'cool', these kids, but they're stuck in the conventional mud. They've got no sense of adventure. He'll be okay when he's picked up with a few mates and sussed out a girl or two."

She stomped back down the steps, calling over her shoulder: "And get him to take those cases up to our room. The removals men are champing at the bit out here and I'll need the passage cleared."

For the next hour, Jack helped with the removals, but with all the rooms, it was the same. He knew what was behind every door. When he pushed through to the kitchen with a box of Dad's precious cooking utensils, he nearly dropped them. The elongated room, with its windows and its back exit leading outside, was exactly as he knew it would be, right down to the cheerless yard and the wall of sheer cliff. There was a heavy mix of honeysuckle and clematis creeping up the wall. He hadn't anticipated that. He also had to admit that, in the confused images infesting his brain, the green-slimed concrete surface and the slate-blue drain in the centre of the yard didn't quite chime, but everything else was just as he knew it would be.

As his dad staggered down the passage with a vacuum cleaner, Mum shouted from the front door, "There's a cupboard under the stairs. The cleaner can go in there." And without thinking, Jack said:

"It's not a cupboard. There's a cellar down there."

His parents were slightly nonplussed because when Dad opened the door, that's exactly how it was.

"How did you know that?" Dad said.

But Jack just shrugged. "Just knew, didn't I?"

He wasn't going to explain. There was no point. His parents wouldn't probe. They were too obsessed with each other and their new house.

Dad was a twenty-first century man – a househusband with far too much of a feminine side for Jack's liking – pernickety about tidiness, with a love of cooking and a domesticity that made Jack cringe.

He wrote the occasional book and articles for some journals and called himself a freelance writer.

It was Mum who earned the cash. She was a doctor, and it was because of her they'd moved to Tregenwyth. She'd been given the post of Medical Registrar at the hospital in nearby Polgarthen, and coming to Cornwall was completely their thing.

They were obsessed with everything about it, from the fishing boats and the white cottages clinging to plunging hills and cliffs, right down to the acres of sea. They loved the quaint pubs and craft shops clustered around the harbours. They loved it all, including this weird, rambling shack that was to be Jack's enforced habitat from now on.

Mum's main reaction to his prediction of a cellar was to ignore it and demand Dad's assistance in moving a dresser, shouting as she blustered through to the dining room: "If there's a cellar, things like the vacuum cleaner can go down there. You can take it down, Jack, and then give the removals men a hand with the settees and the easy chairs. Tell them to put them in the lounge."

The cellar had all the characteristics of any cellar. It was cold and musty, draped with cobwebs and littered with debris. There were dark corners where the single light bulb, the sole source of illumination, never reached.

Dust, dampened to a muddy slime, coated the earth floor and the walls had, at some time, been whitewashed. Now there were huge scars where the whitewash had fallen away and large scabs of encrusted sea-salt seeped through the stonework.

As he stood there, resting the vacuum cleaner by his side, the silence was grim, but then he became aware that it wasn't silence at all.

He thought, at first, it was the sound of blood rushing in his head like you get when you hold a seashell to your ear; but it wasn't. Beneath the cellar floor he could hear the sea. There must be caves down there that led directly to the coast...and all of a sudden, he realised – he'd known there would be caves down there. It had been burned into his memory, but from...when?

It wasn't like déjà vu.

With any kind of déjà vu there was a nagging sensation that something had happened before, but the feeling only came after the thing had happened. With déjà vu he'd never been able to anticipate things, not like he'd been doing since he arrived in Tregenwyth.

Suddenly he dashed up the stairs and out into the passageway, pushing past the removals men.

"I'm going out," he shouted.

"But we need you," Mum yelled. She was calling from the dining room. "There's still more furniture to bring in. There are boxes to store and trunks that need unpacking."

Nothing, though, would induce him to stay in the house a moment longer. "I said I'm going out," he repeated. "I need a break, okay?"

"We've only just come. It's a bit early for a break," Dad said. "Get the unpacking done first, and then we'll all go out."

"It's your house," he retorted. "You do the unpacking. I'm going out *now*."

The removals men looked at each other, but he ignored their knowing nods and their eyes flashing hints about self-willed teenagers and he pushed into the street. "I'll be back to give you a hand when I've had a breather, okay?" he shouted.

It wasn't entirely the breather he'd hoped for though, because the whole village seemed to have the same familiarity. He knew the contours of the cliffs and the dimensions of the harbour. He recognised the smell of the salt in the air and the raucous screech of the seagulls. He was familiar with the way they wheeled and dived. It seemed to be part of his psyche and he couldn't understand why.

He didn't always recognise the details. It was a bit like it had been in the backyard. The rows of brightly embellished shops and the boats rocking in the gentle swell – motor launches, yachts and the fishing boats – and the general feeling of cheerful bustle that always went with a holiday resort, none of these matched what he understood about the place, but the sense of warmth and well-being did ease his anxiety.

He sat on one of the seats positioned around the jetty and let the chatter and laughter of holidaymakers wash over him. The boats were lulled by the undulations of the harbour and he took in their fragmented reflection, glinting a pallet of colour onto the water. He looked at the cottages nestled into the undergrowth of the hillside and somehow, the atmosphere of the place subdued his turbulent mood. It was almost at a level he could manage, and he had to concede that if it wasn't for the sickness of the house, he might possibly get used to living down here. After a while, he was even beginning to figure out what the attraction was for his parents. There was just enough that wasn't familiar to ease the feeling of menace and soon the heat of the sun began to relax his body. He breathed the sea's ozone. It was invigorating, giving him the slightest inkling of wanting to be part of the holiday atmosphere.

But he didn't want to go back to the house.

There was some kind of nightmare going on back there and he couldn't understand anything that was happening. He knew he had to go back though and eventually, he dragged himself away from the seat and climbed the hill.

But as soon as he did, the tall buildings on each side of the road obliterated the magic and warmth of the harbour, the easy-going atmosphere of a seaside resort gave way once more to bleakness, and the feelings of premonition and déjà vu filled his head again.

2

Jack hoped that the intimations of the house would fade as he became more familiar with the place.

Mum began work in Polgarthen and Dad was imposing the O'Hagan touch on everything that surrounded him; cleaning rooms, arranging furniture and establishing himself in the kitchen.

Neither of his parents seemed to have the least inkling of the weird abnormalities that had made such an impact on Jack and for him, all the hopes that familiarity would ease the tensions were dashed daily.

In fact, everything about the house seemed to be careering in the opposite direction. He began to sense there was a knowledge linked to the place that had been burned into his psyche from before he was born and it was as if the building had two existences – the house as it now was and another house – the one in his head, which had the feel of another time about it or else an existence in a parallel world.

As the days groped their way towards the end of the second week, he became even more conscious of the demarcations. The strange 'power' inhabiting the house was intensifying. The feelings weren't tangible, but sometimes, when he walked into a room, he felt as if he'd been ambushed. He sensed the room had been displaced. All Dad's changes were beginning to be familiar enough, with the furniture his parents had brought down from Stevenage arranged to their liking, but the sight sometimes took him by surprise. It felt as if none of it should have been there. He had no vision of what should replace it; it was just that this twenty-first century version of the room was wrong and the force of its incongruity pounded in his head.

Then, one morning, he became aware of three more things about the house, and none of them did anything to ease his tension.

He had been sent to the cellar to fetch the steam floor mop and being sent on such an errand didn't put him in the best of moods because it was clear his father had every intention of forcing him – alpha male from the top of his head to the end of his tightly honed toenails – to use the mop on the kitchen floor. His dignity was feeling violated and he was on a deliberate 'go slow'. He was hoping to win a small victory by riling his pathetic cleanliness-obsessed father. But, if he hadn't been so slow, he might not have noticed that something unusual was going on right under his feet.

As he moved the objects blocking his access to the mop, he was constantly aware of the muffled malaise of sea noises in the caverns. Then … his movements shuddered to a frozen stop. He realised the noises roaring in the background of his consciousness weren't just sea noises. He could hear voices in the cavern – unclear, because of the thickness of rock between him and the caves – but – there were voices, and they were raised and angry. They seemed to go on too, in a tirade that made his blood chill.

In view of the other things that had happened, his first instinct was to suspect what he was hearing might not be real. It may have been part of that other existence …and the very moment he heard the voices, he became convinced that somewhere in the cellar, there was an entrance to those caves. The third discovery came immediately on the heels of this realisation. His eyes glimpsed a key just to his left, hanging from a heavy butcher's nail. He'd never noticed it before and somehow, the sight seemed to encapsulate all the conflict of the house.

It was hanging there in the present, but he knew the butcher's nail must have been rammed into that wall centuries ago. His instinct and his feeling that somewhere, there was an entrance to those caverns, told him this had more to do with the past. He half suspected the key might unlock the entrance and immediately, he grabbed it from the wall and shoved it into his pocket.

Then he stared. He could still hear the voices and he was growing more conscious that these, at least, might not be part of the déjà vu. They seemed more immediate than déjà vu and, and if they were happening now, it meant something was going on in those caves at this very moment; a fact that was as unnerving as all the weird premonitions of the past.

He grabbed the steam mop and made it two-at-a-time out of the cellar.

For the next few days, the noises haunted him. If something was going on down there now, it meant that someone other than his family had access to the caves. He thought of the guy who lived next door, which wasn't a comforting thought.

Jack had glimpsed his next door neighbour on several occasions. He was called Batten. He lived on his own and he had the reputation for being something of a recluse. Whenever Jack saw him striding off down the hill, he sensed there was something not 'quite right' about him.

The three discoveries, along with the other conflicts of the house and this nagging idea that his weird neighbour was conducting some sort of operation in the caverns; made him even more uneasy, and the harbour became an increasingly welcome escape.

On occasions, he would slip away without saying a word. At other times, he would march out quite deliberately, informing his parents that he needed a break. Sometimes, though, he was sent by his dad on some domestic errand.

That's how it was one Monday morning just three weeks after they'd come to Tregenwyth.

His dad had sent him to buy some bits and pieces from the local Spar and emerging from the shadows of the hill and seeing the harbour and bay spread out ahead of him gave him a sense of escape and relief.

He didn't go to Spar immediately. Instead, he found an empty seat at the edge of the jetty where he settled, gazing across at the boats, watching their gentle undulations as water quivered around them.

School had finished for the summer. That was why the harbour was his only means of escape. He was stuck at home all the hours God sent and even though he hated the thought of a new school and the hassle of meeting new people and making new friends, in a way, he wished term hadn't ended. If it hadn't, he wouldn't be with his dad all day, doing chores and running errands and he wouldn't have to be in that house all the time.

His eyes wandered to the headland running west of the harbour, and for a while, he watched cars flashing between gorse bushes and clusters of trees up there.

The sea was limpid blue and the weather was balmy.

Gradually his gaze shifted towards the jetty opposite. There was a boy down there, in the corner of the harbour, working on a small boat. The boat was moored by some steps. He'd seen the boy every time he came down, sorting and untangling his fishing lines. He was bigger than Jack, dark-haired and swarthy. His bare arms were muscular and his frame displayed an adolescent growth that Jack longed for.

As he watched, his hand wandered to his pocket and he pulled out the key he'd found in the cellar. He turned it over in his hand and stared at it. Since the day he'd found it, he always carried it with him for some reason. He didn't quite know what to make of it and his attachment to it puzzled him. But as he pondered the key, the boy glanced in his direction. If Jack ever managed to catch his eye, he always gave him the thumbs up and when he did that, the boy would grin and wave before setting to work on his lines again. He didn't just untangle the lines. Every day when he'd sorted them, he would take an oar and scull out beyond the jetty.

At last, Jack got up and began to wander towards the steps where the boy's boat was moored. He pocketed the key and leaned over the railings, looking down, watching him wrestling with his tangled lines.

The steps down to the boat were in shadow and there were fronds of weed clinging to them. The weed hung from the harbour wall as well and more swirled, bottle green, as the water lapped gently against the jetty.

Even though the boy was cast in the shade, the effort of working left a sheen of sweat on his arms and back. Suddenly, he brushed his hair away from his forehead, dragging a hand across his face and looked up.

"How 'ee doin'?" he said, grinning. "You down 'ere on holiday? I seen 'ee round the place these last few days."

Jack smiled. "No. I'm living up the hill. We've just moved in."

"Bill Burney's place. I know it," the boy said. "They took 'im into an old people's home a couple of years back. Must be a bit run down up there."

"Yeah, it's a dump."

The boy put the line onto a bench that straddled the boat. "Want to come down, do 'ee? Give me a hand with these lines?"

Jack didn't need a second invitation.

"Mind they steps," the boy warned. "The weeds is like grease. One false move and you'll be on your ass." He grinned again as he watched Jack's tentative descent. "I see you aren't used to this kind of thing."

Jack eased himself, grabbing a rope set into the wall. "Not so's you'd notice," he said. "I used to live in Stevenage and there aren't many boats and jetties up there to negotiate."

"Thought you was from up country," the boy said, steadying him. He eased him onto the boat and added, "I'm Terry Blewett – 'Force Ten' to his mates."

"Force Ten?" Jack said. He stretched out both arms in a desperate attempt to maintain a balance.

"Blewett – Force Ten gale. They all call me that. They 'ave done ever since I was in Primary School. What you called?"

Jack staggered again. "Just Jack. No fancy nicknames. Simple Jack O'Hagan, that's me."

"Well, pleased to meet 'ee, simple Jack O'Hagan." Terry held out his hand.

He had a strong handshake, but the movement rocked the boat even more and Jack tumbled to the wooden bench.

"You 'aven't got no sea legs yet, then?" Terry laughed. "Never mind. You just sit where you landed. The sea legs'll come when you been out in the punt a few times."

This was the first moment of genuine ease Jack had experienced. There'd been nothing like it since he'd set foot in Tregenwyth and he welcomed it. For the next half hour, he spent his time wrestling with tangles and sorting lines, getting accustomed to the gentle undulations of the swell. He took in Tregenwyth from its new vantage point. The jetty rose above them and flashes of the other boats reflected in the water. Their colours seemed to melt into the water's movement and there was a constant surround-sound of lapping, along with the slight groan of timbers. All the time he was on the boat, he was aware of being almost at one with the sea, and he loved the sensation.

The smell had a cleansing tang of salt too, and the shops around the harbour looked so different, just breaking the horizon in a benign tranquillity. It was light years away from the predatory terror of the house on the hill.

He worked comfortably, relaxed and chatting.

Terry was the same age as him. It was likely they would be together next term at Polgarthen Academy, and for Jack, things began to look up. It was only when Terry made a suggestion that the magic was broken. "Fancy coming out in the bay now we got the lines sorted? Do a bit of featherin'? Catch a few mackerel?" And immediately, Jack remembered why he was down in the village.

He sighed and looked longingly at the melting horizon beyond the harbour. "I can't," he said. "I've got to get food from Spar for my dad for lunch. I've been gone longer now than I should have been."

A puzzled look flashed across Terry's face and there was a half smile. "For your da? For lunch? Don't your ma do the lunch or haven't you got no mother?"

Jack grinned apologetically. "Mum's a doctor. She works for the Polgarthen Trust. She's a Medical registrar. Dad's a writer and he's around the house all day. He does all the housework."

"What? Cooking and hoovering and things like that?" Terry said.

Jack nodded and a long, low whistle escaped from Terry's lips. "Wouldn't catch me doin' that. Last time I boiled a kettle it caught fire."

"Me too," Jack said. "But that's my dad and there isn't anything I can do about it. He sent me out shopping and I've got to turn up with a bag of groceries. If I don't get the right things, there'll be hell to pay."

He said it with a voice that was light and dismissive, but his heart was sinking. The thought of standing on the doorstep back at the house, with his bag of groceries, was as inviting as an ice bath.

"Think you'd be free tomorrow?" Terry asked and straightaway, Jack's face lit up again.

"You bet. I'll make sure I am."

"Be down 'ere about eleven o'clock then. Get your da to make up a few sandwiches. Tell 'im you'll bring back some mackerel for 'is tea."

"That would be great." Jack staggered to his feet, swaying drunkenly as the boat wobbled.

Terry guided him onto the steps. "Cast off my mooring rope when you're up on the quay, will 'ee?" he said. "Chuck it down and I'll see you, eleven o'clock tomorrow."

Jack watched from the jetty as Terry's muscular frame straddled the stern of the punt. He worked a single oar, propelling himself out towards the harbour entrance and suddenly, the sunlight faded from Jack's soul.

He fetched the groceries and headed for the hill, but as soon as he started to climb, all the gloom of the street – the narrow road, crowded out with dark-faced houses, the dank shadows, sun - starved and still, and the weird premonition that every footstep he took had been taken before – enshrouded him again. It all flooded back.

The murky house frontage seemed to glower and if possible, was worse today. There seemed to be a new hint as he neared the door, as if there was some kind of additional terror to be unleashed.

As he pushed through, all around him he could sense an air of instability. Instantly, he felt for the rusted key in his pocket. He didn't know why he did that, but he'd noticed before that in times of stress, he'd made sure it was there.

He headed down the passage and heard his father bark from the kitchen, "Is that you, Jack?" It was clear his dad wasn't in the best of moods. "Have you had to manufacture those things? It shouldn't have taken you more than ten minutes."

"I met a guy down the harbour, didn't I?" Jack said. "Someone called Terry Blewett. I've been on his boat sorting fishing lines. We've been chatting." He went through to the kitchen, dumping the shopping on the table.

Dad was peeling vegetables at the sink and his weatherworn face looked irritated. "You've been sorting fishing lines with some kid down the harbour?" he snapped. "You'd have been better occupied up in your bedroom sorting that. It's a tip up there. I went up just now and there's no evidence of any floor at all under all your junk."

"I couldn't find anything, could I?" Jack said, slouching to the fridge to grab a can of coke. "Not the way you'd stashed it. Now it's all out, I can lay my hands on anything I want."

"Not without grappling irons, you can't," Dad said. He gave a vicious stab at the potato in his hand. Jack could see his domestic sensibilities had been offended, but he didn't care. His own sensibilities had been offended. He'd been sentenced to live in this dump, and now that he'd spent a bit of time with Terry, the dysfunction of the house had been put into grim perspective.

He remained where he was and he could see his dad's face twist with annoyance.

"Well?" Dad said at last. He was standing, potato peeler in hand immersed in his own world of domesticity, and Jack hated it.

"Well, what?" he said.

"Your belongings upstairs aren't going to get up and find drawers and cupboard space on their own, are they?"

"You mean you want me to put all my things back again?"

"That's the general idea, old son." Dad turned to the draining board and began paring the rest of the skin off the poor, defenceless potato.

Jack waited; but the command had gone out. There was no space for negotiation and finally, he shambled towards the door.

"But I won't be able to find anything," he said.

"If you apply your brain to the task and remember in which repository you placed your things, you'll find everything with ease," his dad snapped. "And you'll have the additional advantage of being able to enter your room without having to resort to flares and a radio beacon."

"Very funny," said Jack.

He made his way to the stairs, but his steps were heavy and his indolence wasn't just fuelled by Dad's blinkered intransigence. His heart was thumping and he could feel that this time, he was actually nervous about going up to his room.

Something was going on. The house seemed to have more attitude and he felt, as he stood outside his bedroom, that this was the portent of something...and he didn't know what.

He sank to the floor, leaning against the wall, staring at the door.

The tension was made worse by the sultry heat. And the sensation of instability all around him was freaking him out. It was as if he'd come to a crisis point, as if the feelings that had possessed him from the very first day had all been building up to this and he didn't know what 'this' was.

His hand went to his pocket again and he grasped the rusted key. It was the second time he'd done that and some instinct told him it was all tied together – the instability, the overpowering apprehension, his attachment to the key; and he had this intangible sense that it would all explode in his face the moment he pushed through to his bedroom.

"I can't hear any action," Dad shouted from the kitchen.

"Just collecting my reserves," called Jack. There was no way he could share what was going on in his head with his father. "Just organising my strategies."

"Good man. I'll be listening for the sounds of implementation then."

"You would," Jack whispered.

But still, he didn't move.

He could hear disturbances in the walls and floorboards, and there was a sound from the hall, like a ticking clock, and that was doubly unnerving because he knew there was no clock in the hall. Nothing about the place was making sense.

The longer he put it off though, the less inclined he would be to turn the handle of his bedroom door, and all this could be tricks of his imagination.

At last, he got up, gripped the handle and turned it.

His eyes were closed and he'd never been more certain of being on the edge of something.

He pushed, breathing deeply and bracing himself. He tried telling himself again that this was irrational, that nothing was going to happen, but then he opened his eyes, bewildered. His door wouldn't move. It must be jammed. Some of his liberated things must have fallen against it.

He tried again, but whatever had fallen, must have been big because the door still wouldn't move. He used his whole body weight and still it wouldn't budge. He stood and stared. He wasn't letting Dad know he couldn't open the door. He didn't need Dad's derision and gloating on top of everything else.

He turned sideways and shoved with his shoulder. But there was no 'give'. It was like pushing at a wall and all around him, the house noises were increasing, groaning and grating. There was the ticking of the clock, and an unearthly roaring like the sea in his ears.

By now he was sweating; not with exertion, but with fear. It occurred to him that there was some force holding the door shut…and the same force seemed to be gripping his body. He was being impelled to barge his way into that bedroom and not just to clear up the mess.

His instinct told him the door must be locked, but there wasn't any keyhole, just a handle.

He gave it another shove and amidst the roaring and the creaks and groans inside his befuddled head, he heard a voice whisper, *"Try the key. Try the key."*

He stood away and brushed his hair back from his forehead. There was no lock.

He couldn't try the key. It would be useless, but he heard the words again. *"Try the key."*

He pushed the key against the solid wood of the door…and it was as if the wood was dissolving. The key sank into the door's surface, and in a trance, he turned it.

Then, even though his mind was screaming that none of this could be happening, he put his shoulder to the door again and pushed.

The door only gave reluctantly. As his body struggled against it, it seemed to be held by a wall of force.

He couldn't prise the door open, and neither could he move away from it.

Then, as though the force was some devouring ectoplasm, it enveloped him, sucking him into the room, suffocating him and swallowing him; he felt that the matter he was being devoured by was shredding and rearranging every cell in his body.

He struggled like someone drowning, fighting for air and then…he was in the room and his mind rocked.

It wasn't his room.

It was the same shape. The window was in the same place, facing him as he stood in the doorway, but none of the things in the room were his. The floor was just bare boards. There was no bed and the furniture was unfamiliar.

By the window were a heavy oak desk and an intricately carved chair. There was a large dresser to his right and a fireplace to his left. Another door by the fireplace led into what had been his parents' bedroom, and while his brain wrestled with this, he realised, to his horror, that the room wasn't the only thing that had changed.

The person who was standing there wasn't him.

The feeling only lasted for a second.

After that, all awareness of himself, of his dad, his mum, everything he knew about the twenty-first century – trains, buses, aeroplanes, space, mobile phones, the Internet, the whole cognisance that was his world was gone.

In its place was a new world and again, it was only new for a second.

Then it slipped like an adjusting lens, and the new awareness was all he'd ever known…and the knowledge that filled his head was no longer Jack O'Hagan's.

The person who was standing there was a girl with a widowed mother down the coast in Penryn and two brothers, the eldest, a farmhand called Thady and the other, Barney, a dragoon who worked with the customs men in Falmouth.

And at that moment, Jack O'Hagan no longer existed.

3

For a while, the girl stood shaking. Something had rocked her mind a few moments ago. She wasn't sure if it was tiredness from being up since before five – or homesickness. She'd only been in service with Mr Trelawny for four weeks and she still longed for her mother and brothers back in Penryn.

It was her brother, Thady, who had found her this position.

Her father had died just after they'd moved from their old home in Holsworthy and everything in Cornwall was so different from what they'd been used to in Devon. With only the meagre income from the two boys, she'd had to get a job.

She missed her mother, though, so much, and her two brothers.

But the feeling she'd just had didn't seem like tiredness or homesickness. When this thing had flooded through her, a weird gibberish had filled her head, more like some kind of brainstorm. It was all over in a second; but it had left her hazy, as if nothing was real.

"Jax!"

She started. She could hear Mrs Spargo, Mr Trelawny's housekeeper, lumbering up the stairs, and in a sudden panic, she turned to check that she'd laid the fire and cleaned the room properly.

"Jax! In the Lord's name, where are you, girl?" Mrs Spargo shouted.

Jax was *her* name. At home they called her Martha; but here, in service, it was the cold formality of her family name.

"I'm in the master's dressing room," she called.

Mrs Spargo came panting up the stairs. She was plump and ruddy, with grey hair curling from under her cloth cap. She snapped, "There you are, child. It's no fun draggin' yourself up all these stairs at my age." Her face was creased with impatience. "And look at yourself, for Goodness' sake. The master wants you in the drawing room, and you're standin' there with soot all over your face."

Jax drew an arm across her cheek, and Mrs Spargo aimed a slap at her wrist.

"Don't do that! Where's your sense girl? Just look at your sleeve now." She took a hanky and began rubbing the stain. "Goodness knows what he wants you for." She stepped back and scanned Jax for further tell-tale marks. Then she grunted, "You'll do. Now get down to the drawin' room double quick."

Jax crept down the stairs, trembling. She couldn't imagine what she'd done to be summoned to Mr Trelawny's drawing room. He'd hardly spoken to her since she'd started working at the house.

When she got to the door, she knocked and her knuckles barely made a sound, but she heard a harsh voice rasping, "Enter," from the other side, and she pushed through.

Mr Trelawny had his back to her. He was sitting facing the fire and the pillbox cap he wore when he wasn't wearing his wig was all that showed above the chair. There was a skein of tobacco smoke creeping above his head, and as she stood there, his arm appeared from around the chair, beckoning.

"Come round 'ere, child," he said.

He was a heavy man with a florid face, and the white hair hung loose, fringing his smoker's cap. There were tufts of bristle in his ears, and he squinted myopically. "Right round," he said.

She shuffled towards him, one hand gripping the other, tense with anxiety and for a moment, he just stared at her. Then he barked, "Settlin' in all right, are you?"

She nodded and his mouth clicked irritably.

"'Aven't you got no tongue, cheel?"

"I'm settlin' in all right, sir, thank you," she whispered.

He craned his head and peered at her again. "Can you sing?" he said suddenly and she blushed, taking a step back. She didn't think this was a proper question for him to be asking, but she said again in a low voice:

"My brother, Barney, he says I can, sir. He says I've got a voice like an angel."

Mr Trelawny took the pipe from his mouth and coughed deep in his throat. "I've heard you," he said. "Singin' round the place." Then he leaned forward, peering more intently. "Turn around then, girl. Let's 'ave a proper look at you." He prised himself into a standing position, staggering slightly, and it made her jump. "I aren't goin' to hurt you," he said. "There isn't no need to be scared."

He hobbled over to where she stood, and drew her firmly by the chin so that he was looking straight into her eyes. "Now, child. How clever are you? D'you think you could learn a song for me, words and tune?"

She gulped and nodded. She was frightened and confused. Nobody had told her that being in service would involve learning songs.

"The words might be strange to 'ee, mind, though the tune's simple enough."

He let her go and shuffled to the other end of the room where he picked up a piece of white cloth draped over a chair. It was a long, formless cloak with a hood.

"Put this on," he said. "You'll need it for when you're singin'. Special it is."

All this seemed so wrong and she could feel herself fainting away. She grabbed the back of a chair for support, but she dared not say anything and with shaking fingers, she put on the cloak.

There was some kind of a keyboard in the window and as she draped herself, he led her over to it.

She couldn't understand why he was making her do this. Her heart was thumping and she could feel her legs going weak again. Was it some kind of witchcraft he was involved in? Was he planning to make her take part in wicked practices?

Hesitantly, he picked out a tune on the keyboard, jabbing at the keys with one finger and she wished with all her soul that she was back at home with her mother and Thady and Barney. It was a tune she'd never heard before, but the melody was gentle, like a seabird in flight, simple and easy to learn. She had no difficulty singing the notes back to him.

"That's good, cheel. Now I'll teach you the words," he said, and he began to chant in a flat, tuneless drawl, following the song's rhythm. But as he chanted, the blood ran cold inside her. The words that came out of his mouth held no meaning.

It was witchcraft for certain.

She repeated the words, wide-eyed with apprehension.

"Ow huv-kolon gwra dos. A ny glewydh y'n koos,
An eos ow kana pur hweg?
A ny glewydh hy lev, a woles a sev
Y'n nansow ow kana mar deg?"

She was so scared, breathing was difficult. "What are you makin' me do?" she whispered.

But that just made him swing around, and she could see a glint of threat burning in his eye. "Just mind your business, child, and do what you're told, that's all," he snapped. "Now, sing they words back to me."

She wanted to cry and she dared not ask him anything more. She stumbled over the unfamiliar chant, hiding her fear as well as she could, and she struggled to match the words to the notes. *"Ow huv-kolon gwra dos..."*

She sang them over and over, until they were firmly in her head.

Then there were more verses, all with the same meaningless jumble of words, and there wasn't a syllable of sense to any of them.

Fear made her quick though, and within an hour, she'd learned the whole song by heart, and Mr Trelawny seemed pleased. He put a hand on her shoulder. "Good," he said. "Now, tonight, I've got a job for you with that cloak and the song. It'll mean a sovereign for 'ee if you do it right; but if you start askin' questions, or goin' your own way, all you'll get is a whippin'. Do you get my meanin'?"

He took the cloak and bundled it into a drawer in the bureau. "Now, I want for you to serve dinner for me this evenin'," he said. "And then, when you've cleared away, you come back 'ere and I'll tell you what I want for you to do."

She scurried from the room and for the rest of the day she couldn't get any of it out of her head – the song, Mr Trelawny wanting to see her again this evening, the threats, the promises. By the time dinner was over and she'd crept back to her room in the attic, her brain was in turmoil.

There was a battered panel of brass on her bedroom door. She used it as a mirror and as she peered into it, what she saw made her shudder. Her hair was a mess of spiralling strands. It twisted and curled to her shoulders, and it was as ginger as saffron. Her face was milky pale...and her eyes...Barney said there was a tinge of green in her eyes. Green for witchcraft, she thought.

She dragged her fingers through her curls, tidying herself as best she could. Then she glanced at the shadowy face again. Her nose was small; not a witch's nose; but the face...and the thin mouth...the sallow skin...with a black coat and a stooped back, she'd pass for a witch.

When she was ready, she groped her way down the stairs and through the passageway to where Mr Trelawny was waiting in the drawing room. He had his wig on now and a heavy greatcoat that made his bulky frame look even more imposing.

"We'll be goin' out on the cliffs," he said. He hobbled to the bureau and removed the linen cloak, thrusting it towards her. Then he took a walking cane from the rack in the hall and added, "I'll tell you what I want for you to do as we go. And you listen careful, mind. You do one bit of this wrong and it'll mess up the whole night's work for a lot of people."

4

It was dark and cold outside and it was hard to pick her way on the cobbles as she followed Mr Trelawny's black shape down the hill. He strode out towards the quayside; and as the bay opened ahead of them, hints of moonlight lit the harbour. There were men down there, lots of them, working on a shallow- bottomed galley and doing strange things to a group of ponies. They were harnessing them and washing them down, and they were rubbing them with what seemed like soap or grease.

Mr Trelawny stared at the men as he passed and they nodded, doffing their caps, and it was as if Jax was in some sort of nightmare. No one spoke. They just acknowledged his presence in a hushed silence and carried on with their work.

He turned up onto the west cliff. She had to struggle to keep up with him because he climbed so quickly, stabbing his cane into the damp turf to give him leverage, and as they climbed, he barked a string of instructions at her.

Nothing he said made her feel any better. The song was a charm, he said. There was a cutter coming in and her singing would bring it to safety. She had to walk along the cliff all night, singing without stopping. If she stopped or talked to anyone, then she knew what she'd get.

She didn't understand. Why would any ship need a song to bring it to safety and why was it coming in at night? Why were so many men doing things down on the jetty? Why did she have to be dressed in this weird white cloak?

But she dared not ask any questions. She'd already seen what Mr Trelawny was like when she asked questions.

She clung to every word he said though, because he'd told her…if she did one bit wrong…she couldn't bring herself to think what would happen to her if she made a mistake.

Eventually, they reached a rough stone wall at the top of the headland and he left her, grunting more directions as he went.

Ahead of her, a dark wood loomed, deep in shadows, and she shivered. Singing at night to bring luck to a boat *was* some kind of witchcraft. It *was* wicked practices he was making her do. Everything about it was wrong and she felt lonely and afraid. This wasn't what she'd expected when she went into service. It was dangerous. Thady and her mother had persuaded her to take this position. But, thinking of them and Barney made her throat ache, and tears stung the backs of her eyes. She knew she had to put her family out of her head.

In the faint light of the waxing moon, she could just make out the two peninsulas, Dodman Point to her left and St Anthony Head to her right. Beyond St Anthony, she thought, were the river Fal, and an inlet that led to Penryn. But she must not think of that. She must concentrate.

She stood, remembering the string of instructions Mr Trelawny had barked at her. Then, far out on the water, she made out the spectral shape of a boat. It was moving darkly towards land. That would be Mr Trelawny's cutter.

She stepped onto the cliff path, putting the white cloak on as she went and for a while, she followed the path's meandering course between the gnarled and twisted trunks of the trees. She only got a glimpse of the water and she wondered if there would be any point in singing if she was hidden from the boat. But Mr Trelawny had told her to sing the song all the time she was on the cliff, so, scared as she was, she pulled the cloak around her and began to sing with all the strength she could muster.

"Ow huv-kolon gwra dos,
A ny glewydh y'n koos,
An eos ow kana pur hweg?"

And all the time she was groping through the trees, stumbling on the uneven path until it opened onto a ledge. A narrow valley led up to a rough downland to her right. Below her was an inlet, and there were things going on down there she could never have dreamed of. The cove seemed alive with the black shapes of men and ponies. The flat-bottomed galley was moored out by the cutter, and she could see men from the galley swarming all over the bigger boat.

As she watched, she was so overcome that for a moment, she forgot to sing and then panic gripped her. Mr Trelawny had said she mustn't stop for an instant. Immediately she set off again and this time, she sang more loudly, trying to make up for the silence.

"A ny glewydh hy lev a woles a sev,
Y'n nansow ow kana mar deg?"

All night she walked, backwards and forwards across the cliffs, singing until her throat ached.

Finally, the cutter went free, and the black etched galley came ashore on muffled oars. There would be no respite though, not until Mr Trelawny fetched her, and as the night wore on, her fear grew because she was conscious that she wasn't alone on the cliff. In the scrubland beyond her, there were shadows – men hiding, men waiting, and she couldn't grasp what was happening.

Her head was in a fog of confusion and all the time, with those shadows hovering, she felt more and more threatened.

Then, as she reached the headland and the cove again, someone called out from the scrub above her and she froze. The voice shouted, "Martha, is that you down there?" She knew whose voice it was.

It was Barney, her brother, the coastguards' dragoon from Falmouth, and as soon as he called, someone yelled from further down the cliff-side. For a moment she caught a glimpse of her brother, standing on the rising downland with his sword drawn.

Then there were footsteps all around her. Shapes pounded up the hill, and stones rained down. Shadows beyond the trees materialised into men, and they were shouting, brandishing clubs. Someone threw a stick that knocked the sword out of her brother's hand. She watched him scramble across the ground, searching to retrieve it. Then he staggered to his feet and ran across the downland towards the valley. But he was pursued by the men wielding their clubs, and towards Tregenwyth, another group of men lit a fire while torchlight traced frenzied paths across the beach.

She stood there, paralysed…and she waited until the baying for her brother had faded into shadows and the figures on the cliff had melted back into the darkness.

Now, apart from a whisper in the offshore wind and the wash of the waves, there was nothing. The ship had gone and the sea was a vast stretch of empty swell.

She couldn't move, but then, out of the dull confusion in her muddied head, a thought crept in, and it dismayed her even more. If that rabble ever caught her brother, they'd kill him. She had to do something to save him, and forgetting everything Mr Trelawny had said, she scrambled up towards the downland, struggling in the direction of the valley where the men had gone in pursuit.

But as she groped, something barred her way. A heavy shadow towered ahead of her and white terror flashed in her eyes as a harsh voice growled, "And where do you think you're off to, cheel?"

It was Mr Trelawny. Even in the darkness, she could make out his features. He was grim, his powdered wig shadowing his face, his eyes staring down at her, and for a second, her brain went blank. Then she gasped, "I was just comin' to find you, sir. When they lit those fires and ran like that, I was scared you'd leave me out 'ere on my own."

"I told you to sing 'til I came," he snapped. "I said you was to wait for me in the woods."

"I was scared," she said again, but his grip on her shoulder tightened and he glared into her face.

"Did you see any fighting up here, girl?" he said, and somehow she knew her life depended on how she replied.

"I saw a soldier. The men went after 'im."

"Dragoons," Mr Trelawny sniffed. "Customs' shore men. Was there many of them, cheel?"

She had a wicked ache in her throat and it was hard to keep her voice steady. "Only one," she whispered, wiping a sleeve across her eyes. "A boy. They went after him with clubs."

He scanned the headland and grunted, "I hope they gived 'im a damned good hiding."

He didn't say another word as they climbed down the cliff and crossed the quayside.

When they reached the front door, he took the white cloak and pressed something metallic into her hand.

But her eyes were stinging with tears as she closed her fingers around it.

She knew what he'd given her.

Her brother was out there on the cliff, lying dead by now for all she knew. And if he was dead, she'd done her bit towards killing him. He wouldn't have called if he hadn't recognised her voice. She was holding blood money in her hand.

She could hardly drag herself up the stairs, and she couldn't begin to grasp what she was involved in.

Exhausted, she fell onto her bed and the attic door swung shut.

She heard it click. But as it closed, something else, something beyond all that was natural, began to happen.

A power started tearing at her body, dragging her out of herself. It seemed to be pulling her off her bed, shredding her, ripping her to pieces, taking her through the closed door, buffeting her, sending her tumbling. And every jolt jarred in her bones until she collapsed against the wall opposite Mr Trelawny's dressing room ...and in a moment of terrifying disorientation, Jack O'Hagan opened his eyes and shook himself in disbelief.

5

He was slumped against the wall and it felt as though he'd been thrown there by some mammoth force.

It was hard to remember exactly what had happened. He knew he'd been trying to get into his bedroom, but...then everything had turned to chaos.

There'd been a kind of resistance when he'd tried the door. He remembered that. He remembered having to push at it – really shove, and it was then that everything went crazy.

He didn't know what, but something mad seemed to have happened.

All he could be sure about was that the tensions and the feelings around the house had gathered into a demonic force which had thrust him against the wall...and yet...in his head there was more.

There was a weird feeling that between the time he'd shoved at the door and now, a window had opened onto another age. The memory was chaotic, but there were bits that were clearer and there'd been a kind of fear. There'd been a panorama that had taken him beyond the house, and he was conscious of names. But he couldn't recall any of them or the places. It was like clutching at dreams, and the whole mosaic was fading even as he struggled to recall it. Within a few moments, all that was left was this out-of-body feeling as if nothing around him was real.

He repositioned himself and then he began to tremble. It was all down to the house. Now it had found an even more menacing way to get at him. It was taking him over and he hated it.

He shut his eyes and wondered if he was going mad. He couldn't even remember why he was trying to open his door in the first place.

What was he doing on the stairs? What was so urgent that he had to get into his bedroom?

He tried steady breathing in an attempt to calm himself and then, from the passage, he heard footsteps, and the footsteps made him remember why he was here.

"Have you still not started on that room?" a voice shouted. His dad was lumbering up the stairs and Jack opened his eyes just in time to see his father, hyperactive with irritation, lines of impatience on his face. He was bounding towards him; but when he caught sight of where he was, he stopped and the lines softened to a puzzled concern.

"Are you all right, Jack, old boy?" he said.

Jack moved gingerly. His bones were aching. The force must have packed a massive punch. Cautiously, he leaned forward, attempting to drag himself to his feet.

"Did you trip or something?" His dad knelt on the stairs, looking anxiously into his face. He ran a hand over his legs and arms. "No bones broken. But how did you finish up in a heap like this?"

"I don't know."

"Did you pass out or something?"

"I said, I don't know." His dad was fussing like a mother hen and he could do without that. "I just found myself in this heap on the floor, okay?"

He struggled to his feet and as he did so, the rusted key fell to the ground. He'd been gripping it for all he was worth, and at the back of his mind, there was some crazy notion that it was a sovereign.

"What's that?" Dad said.

Jack grabbed it and pushed it back into his pocket. "It's nothing. It's some old thing I found hanging in the cellar. I thought it might unlock a door somewhere."

"Your bedroom door?" Dad said. He glanced up and chuckled. "That's a bit of wishful thinking, son. You can't find a key to lock that. There's no keyhole, so don't get any ideas about telling me you've cleaned up in there and then denying me access to check."

"I know there's no keyhole," Jack said. "I don't know why I had the key in my hand."

Dad put a consoling hand on his shoulder. "It must have been too much sun this morning, sitting in that chap's boat."

"He isn't a chap, he's Terry Blewett," said Jack. "And his boat was moored under the jetty. It was in the shade."

"Well." Dad looked at him again and then across at the closed door. "Whatever it was, you seem to be over it, so now I'm up here, how about I give you a hand with the tidying up?"

He stepped across the landing, gripping the door handle and immediately, Jack grabbed him, pulling him away. For a moment his dad looked puzzled, but at the same time, he laughed. "Don't tell me you've developed an abhorrence of muddle in your old age," he said. "It may be a mess in there, but it's not irretrievable."

He turned the handle again and instantly Jack put an arm across his face...but nothing happened. The door swung open to reveal a bedroom exposing all of his organised chaos, with the divan and cupboards and the IKEA chest of drawers. It was just as he'd left it that morning, and the sight of the normality jolted him. For some reason, he wasn't expecting it.

"Half an hour of concentrated effort and we'll have this lot transformed," Dad said.

"Yeah. And unless I watch every move you make, I'll be back where I started. I won't know where anything is."

Dad turned to him, and he looked irritated again. "Look son, do you want me to help you or not?"

"It's okay," Jack said. "You go down and carry on with whatever in the kitchen. I'll sort this lot my way."

"As long as your way doesn't involve the use of floor space to stack your belongings," said Dad. He began to retreat down the stairs. "And if you feel faint again, for goodness sake, give your old dad a shout, eh?"

"I'll be all right," Jack said.

But he felt nervous as he stepped into his room and all the time he was there, he made sure the door stayed firmly open.

When his mother came home that evening, she instigated an inquest. He'd expected that, and he'd expected it to be clinical and business-like because that was how his mum was. She was a large woman with a knack for making everyone know she was there. Her hair was auburn, short and cut in a style that had no style. Her face and body were big and blustering and she was always animated by a super-sized efficiency. Even her sense of humour was oversized. It was as if her tongue was a lash, driving everything ahead of it. That was how she got on, Dad said. It was her dynamic no-nonsense personality.

"Dad tells me you took a bit of a tumble this morning," she said. They were settling around the table in the dining room for dinner. Both his parents insisted on eating in the dining room. Dinner was a social occasion they said, not some opportunity to sprawl in front of the television with trays.

"It wasn't anything," he said, but his mum wasn't going to be fobbed off.

"What a ridiculous thing to say," she snapped. "You collapsed on the stairs and that's something and it needs looking at. Did you feel faint or dizzy before you fell? Did you have a headache?"

"No," Jack said. "I probably tripped on one of the steps. It's so dark up there and those stairs twist like a drunken screw. There isn't one step that's the same width as the next and some of the floorboards are loose."

His mum smiled. "True, but I want to take a look at you all the same."

She came over, giving him a quick assessment with her eyes and then she felt his limbs. After that, she had his tongue out and did the finger test on his vision.

He resisted every move. There was nothing wrong with him. He knew it was the house, but neither of his parents would be ready for that kind of information.

"Lay off," he said. "This is supposed to be dinner, not your surgery."

"Well, if you'd prefer, I'll have you in hospital tomorrow and check you over, there," she said.

Immediately he backed off. Tomorrow it was Terry and the punt and nothing was going to stand in the way of that. Besides, he hated hospitals.

When his mum had satisfied herself he was all right she shrugged and said, "I suggest you take more water with it next time." Then she returned to her dinner.

Jack chuckled. "Chance would be a fine thing."

But they weren't going to let things drop. Mum glanced at Dad and Dad leaned back in his chair.

"You know, Jacky boy," he said. "We do realise it's difficult for you down here, leaving all your mates in Stevenage and having to uproot. And it's the school holidays so you're not getting chances to meet people of your own age."

"I met Terry Blewett," Jack said. "I'm going fishing with him tomorrow."

But with his parents, it was always the same. If either of their mouths were heading somewhere, the mouth pressed on blindly until it reached its destination. Dad hardly heard what he said about Terry. He just trundled on with his own pre-ordained agenda.

"I had a chat with our neighbour this afternoon," he said and Jack started.

"You chatted to Batten?"

"Mr Batten, yes. He runs the local choir, you know? And he's got places for good trebles."

"You're joking. You want me to join a choir run by that creep?"

"You know you've got a great voice," said Mum. "You should give it an airing and there are a few young folk in the choir. It would be an opportunity to meet people, and it would be something to do."

"If I was that desperate for something to do, I'd find someone to pull my toenails out," he said. "Batten's weird."

"You don't know that, and it's a good choir," Dad persisted. "You could make a bit of money singing at weddings and Bar mitzvahs."

Mum sniffed. "Well, probably not Bar mitzvahs, considering it's a Church of England choir."

"But I don't believe in God," Jack said. "I don't want to go singing hymns in some choir. For one thing, it would mean I'd have to go to church every Sunday."

"Well, we think you should," said Dad. "It would get you out of yourself."

This time, though, he wasn't open to negotiation. "No way," he said. "Not with that guy Batten in charge. I'll stick with Terry Blewett, if it's all the same to you. Besides, it's a lot more fun fishing with Terry than it would be singing hymns in some choir, especially one that's run by that creep."

"But I've told him you'll join," Dad said.

"Well, you can untell him," said Jack. He stared at his food and whatever appetite he'd had for Carbonnade of Beef was dissipating fast.

At last, he got up.

"Where are you going?" Dad demanded.

"Out," he said.

"But we haven't finished dinner."

"I have," said Jack. "The thought of joining Batten's choir has killed my appetite. I just want space and fresh air, okay?"

He saw Mum glance at his dad and shake her head. He didn't give them time to say anything more. He just headed for the door and out into the street.

He wanted a break from the pressure and he wanted to be free of this overbearing house; but it didn't turn out like that.

His head was still filled with confusion from this morning, and when he pushed through the door into the street, for a moment, his senses were jarred. The sight of the smooth tarmac took him by surprise. He could have sworn the street was cobbled and for a few seconds, he felt totally disorientated.

Then he staggered down the steps to the pavement, shaking the dislocation out of his head. Perhaps he *was* going mad. When they'd arrived a few weeks earlier, the car would have been shaken to its rivets if it had been driven over cobbles. He would have remembered, and it had been a smooth ride, so why did he have it in his mind that the hill was cobbled?

It taunted him all the way down to the harbour, and there were other off-balance assumptions. When he arrived at the bottom of the hill, the harbour, with its ribbon of shops and pubs, the garish canopies, the festooned shop-windows and cluttered pavements, the souvenir displays and beach-ware, the ice-cream parlours and the seaside cafes, all seemed to crowd the quay even more unnaturally than usual. There was a layer in his head that was convinced there'd be a more austere harbour.

He found an empty bench and sat down, watching the movement of the moored boats. The tide was lower than it had been this morning and below him, the harbour bed was laced with dried husks of seaweed. They littered the sun-baked silt as the encroaching water lapped at the sand driven by the incoming tide.

He tried filling his lungs with the ocean air, but no matter how many gulps of ozone he inhaled, it didn't seem to be helping. He couldn't feel at one with the tourists or with the locals out for their evening stroll. His head was plagued with a discordant stream of contradictions, totally out of kilter with what was going on around him and he couldn't pin any of them down. As he sat there, the feelings swamped him, dragging him so deeply into his own thoughts that he almost leapt out of his body when a grime-encrusted hand gripped his shoulder and a gravelly voice said: "Watchya, simple Jack."

Terry was standing behind him, grinning, and Jack's face lit into a smile. He made room on the bench. "Watchya, Force Ten," he said.

Terry sat down. He had a bag of chips and he thrust it under Jack's nose.

Jack took one of the chips. "Where did you get these?" he said. "I might get some later." The act of eating brought something more like normality to him and if he was honest, he was ravenous. He'd hardly touched Dad's Carbonnade of Beef.

"Eat as many as you like," Terry said. "I bought more than I could manage."

Jack grabbed a handful and that made Terry chuckle. "Be careful mind," he warned. "The gulls is wicked around here, especially when they see a handful of chips. They'll dive-bomb 'ee and they'll have that lot off you as soon as look at you."

Jack shoved all but one back into the bag hurriedly. "Sorry," he said. "But I'm starving, to be honest. I hardly ate any of Dad's tea. I'll take them one at a time. You not out fishing then?"

"I wouldn't be 'ere talkin' to you if I was," Terry laughed. "Not unless there was two of me. You still on for tomorrow?"

"You try stopping me."

"Don't often see you down 'ere this time of night," Terry said.

Jack took another couple of chips. "Had a row at home, didn't I?" he said. "I had to get out to clear my head."

"Tell me about it. My da's a past master at windin' me up. I reckon, before they're allowed to have kids, they 'ave to take degrees in it."

Jack nodded. "Trouble is, they will do their thing. They don't consult you and then they expect you to agree to all their rubbish like you didn't have any opinions of your own."

"What your lot done now?" Terry said. He pushed the bag towards him again. "You can 'ave the lot. I got chips pokin' out between my ribs, I've 'ad so many."

Jack took the bag and bit into a chip, watching the circling gulls warily. They were already wheeling around with menacing intent, and filling the bay with echoes of their guttural cries. "The guy next door to us, he runs the church choir and the idiots have only told him I'd join."

"Batty Batten?" Terry said. " 'Ee do live up your way, don't 'ee? You want to watch 'im though. 'Ee's as bent as a hair grip."

"The guy's a total weirdo," Jack said. "And there is no way I'm joining a choir run by him."

Terry leaned back on the seat. "It isn't just that though," he said. "I mean it's the way 'ee do go around the place. 'Ave you seen 'im? It's like the guy's got somethin' on his mind – like 'ee's always lookin' over 'is shoulder. I wouldn't trust 'im no further than I could spit. 'Ee's got a guilty secret, I reckon."

"That's exactly what I thought when I saw him. He's dead unfriendly. I've never seen him speak to anyone and

I can't imagine how he got to be in charge of a church choir."

"They're a funny lot, they church people," Terry said. "But I got to hand it to 'im. He do a good job with that choir. They're always winnin' prizes and cups and things."

Jack took another couple of chips. He was hurrying through them now because the gulls seemed to be amassing in a serious battle formation, squawking messages to their accomplices that they'd happened on this fool on the quayside with a bag of chips and no clue as to how to handle them. He could see their beady eyes looking at the bag and they were swooping with that determined air. He covered the chips and Terry laughed.

"You won't stop them like that," he said. "They'll knock your hand out the way quicker than you can duck. Best thing is to start walkin'. If we stay sittin' 'ere they'll 'ave the lot, and we'll get shat on into the bargain."

They got up and the gulls scattered, screeching with indignation, sending their raucous cries echoing. "What do you think Batten's up to then?" Jack said.

"I don't know. It's just, 'ee's so shifty."

They strolled across the jetty. "Everybody thinks he's up to something and 'ee's got a wicked manner with him." Suddenly, he stopped, breathed sharply, digging at Jack's ribs and whispered, "Talk of the devil."

He nodded towards the other side of the road and there, stout, with his skimpy strands of hair flying wild from his head was Batten. He seemed to be rushing, glancing over his shoulder and making for the cliff road and the headland.

"How shifty is that?" Terry whispered. "'Ee goes off up there every night, pretty near. And you can't tell me that guy's out for an evening stroll."

Jack nodded. "It's well weird," he said.

"Want to follow 'im, do 'ee? See what 'ee's up to. I wouldn't go on my own, but you and me together…"

Jack wasn't sure he wanted to. He couldn't get away from the menace of what had happened earlier and his instincts told him pursuing Batten would add to his troubles.

He shook his head and Terry said, "I wasn't planning on confronting the guy. I just thought we could follow him to see where 'ee goes." But already Batten was nearing the top of the cliff path. He kept glancing back, even though there was no one else on the hill. There was no point in setting off in pursuit. There weren't many places where they could conceal themselves and he was too far ahead.

"We're not going to catch him up there tonight, not now he's that far up the hill," Jack said.

Terry shrugged. "I reckon we'd lose 'im on the cliff anyway, 'ee's beltin' on so fast."

"We could give it a go tomorrow, if he does it every night."

They shunted themselves onto the harbour wall and Jack finished the chips. This talk about Batten had made him feel unsettled again. Batten was shifty. Terry reckoned he was into something bad and Jack couldn't get the voices he'd heard in the caverns below his cellar out if his head. "If the guy is up to something, do you think he's doing things from his house?" he said. "I heard noises under our cellar a few days ago. Talking and shouting. There are caves down there running in from the sea. You can hear the waves washing in."

"Yeah, I've 'eard about the caves," Terry said. "But those voices? Was they on Batten's side of the house?"

Jack nodded. "I think so."

"More than likely, it's 'im then. I seen enough of 'im to know 'ee's up to something."

"Do you think he could be using the choir as a cover for what he's doing?" said Jack.

"Wouldn't surprise me."

Jack stared at the boats as the incoming tide crept around them. "Perhaps I'll join the choir after all," he said. "If I did that, it would be like infiltrating whatever he's doing – only until I've found out what's going on though." He looked at Terry. Somehow Terry gave him confidence. "Why don't you join, too? It would be better, both of us being there."

Terry shook his head and grinned. " 'Ave you 'eard me sing? I got a voice like a crow with laryngitis. Anyway, I'd rather do a couple of rounds in a dentist's chair than join Batten's choir."

They stayed on the jetty, chatting until dusk crept across the bay and the harbour transformed itself with skeins of lights and the garish illumination of the shops. Jack was feeling better, but as he said goodbye to Terry and began to climb the hill for home, he suddenly felt alone. The darkness seemed to nurse a threatening gloom. It had an uneasy feel about it and there were sounds. They weren't coming from the tarmac road either. They seemed to be created by a harsher surface, as if there were footsteps on cobbled stones, and behind him, he sensed a stick tapping. He was certain he was alone in the street, but he could still hear the sounds and they made the hair on the nape of his neck rise.

By the time he'd reached his house, the force was even stronger and as he pushed through the front door, he was swamped by premonitions.

Mum and Dad were in the lounge and he knew, for them, life was just trundling by as usual. He found engaging with them an effort. He didn't tell them he'd decided to join the choir, and he couldn't concentrate on Dad's plans for redecorating the hall. After a while, he excused himself and went to his room.

But that made him even more uneasy. There was the memory of opening his door earlier.

His bedroom was a hostile place.

And that night, he didn't feel comfortable as he got ready for bed.

6

Nothing unusual happened, but all night something wasn't quite in gear. His dreams followed a wayward path, as if they were trying to recreate what had happened when he went in to tidy his room. When he woke, he couldn't recall any of the details. It was just this nagging sense that he'd experienced a disjointed re-arrangement of time and as he got up to face breakfast, he felt as though he'd been dragged through thorn bushes, and his head was heavy with exhaustion.

His surliness annoyed his dad.

Mum was more dismissive. "Teenage strop," she said. "It's no good fighting it. He's got to grow through it." That aggravated him. It all sounded so enlightened, but he knew these were just neat expressions she turned out so she didn't have to discover the real reason for his mood.

"It's all very well for you to say that," his dad said. "You don't have to live with him all day."

Jack shoved a spoon around his bowl of muesli and stared at the table. "Well, you won't have to live with me today, will you?" he said. "I'm out with Terry, fishing, and it's not teenage strop. I'm tired because I had creepy dreams all night. This house is doing my head in."

Mum sniffed and began collecting her gear for work. "It's got nothing to do with the house, Jack. It's teenage strop. You'll grow through it."

Dad got up and gathered the breakfast things from the table. "If you're going to be out all day," he said, "I suppose you'll be wanting a packed lunch?"

"Yeah, right," said Jack. "You do that. I'm going up to get ready. I'll pick the food up on my way out."

He loped off to his bedroom, but he still couldn't get the previous day out of his head. He felt a pang of anxiety as he pushed at his door. Since the incident with it yesterday morning, the fear was always there that there'd be another performance of the crazy madness.

He didn't know what he was meant to wear for fishing, but he didn't have the gear to dress up as a fisherman, so it was just trainers, jeans and a T-shirt. It looked as if it was going to be a hot day and jeans and T-shirt were all Terry ever wore.

He picked up his lunch and Dad did his usual mother hen act. "Shouldn't you be taking a sweater or something? If you're out in the bay, the breezes can be a bit nippy."

"I'll take a hoodie," Jack said. Then, as he left, just for the sake of devilment, he shouted over his shoulder, "By the way, I'm going to join Batty Batten's choir after all."

As soon as he'd said it, he shut the door, blocking out Dad's exclamations of confusion, and he chuckled. He'd done something to keep Dad happy. He wasn't all bad.

The harbour was bustling, and the morning sunlight lifted his spirits enough to make him swing his holdall over his shoulder with an air of nonchalance. Terry was already on the punt and he looked up and grinned.

"You're early," he said.

"Shows how keen I am, doesn't it?" said Jack.

He negotiated the descent. The weeds growing across the granite steps were slippery and he didn't have the sure-footed confidence of a local.

" 'Ere, give us your 'and," Terry said. "And stand firm." He gripped hold of Jack's arm and pulled the punt closer to the steps so he could walk across, but as Jack placed his foot on the deck, everything rocked. He threw out his arms to steady himself and Terry laughed. "You 'aven't developed no sea-legs overnight then?" he said.

"I have," Jack said. "Only, I've got this holdall. That's what's putting me off balance."

"Yeah, sure," said Terry. "You park your ass somewhere and stay put. I don't want to be going up your da's later to tell 'im you got drowned falling out of the punt."

"Haven't you got life-jackets?" Jack said and that made Terry laugh again.

"This isn't no cruise ship you great land-lubber," he said. "I'd be the laughing stock if I went out carrying life jackets. You just sit down and stay put, that'll be good enough."

They worked on the lines for an hour or more, sorting and untangling them, then layering them into a basket, attaching the barbed hooks to a rim of cork. Each hook was fixed with a brightly coloured feather and Jack frowned questioningly. "What are they for?" he asked.

"They look like tiddlers in the water. The mackerel think they're small-fry. They try to eat them and then they're caught on the hooks."

"That's cruel, isn't it?" Jack said, screwing up his face, and Terry grinned.

"What planet are you from? That's the way we catch fish, that and nets. You like to eat fish, you got to catch them."

Jack worked at the lines and as he did so, he took in the harbour. He had the same feeling as yesterday, almost as though he was part of the water, with the limpid light and the splinters of colour all around and the cool breath of salt cleansing his nostrils.

"I love this," he said.

"You wait till we get out in the bay," said Terry. "There isn't nothing like it."

Jack was sent up to cast off and he tried the steps without the support rope this time. In his own opinion, he did a decent job too. Terry made his way to the back of the punt, grabbing the oar and straddling the width of the boat, and there was a gentle rocking as it nosed through to the harbour entrance.

The jetty slid past and the perspective of the quay and shops inched away. This was magic, the sun, the sea, the blue of the sky and the caressing breeze. The other Tregenwyth and the torments of the house seemed miles away.

At ease with himself, Jack lay in the bow, trailing a hand in the water, until Terry said: "You don't want to be doing that." He was laughing again. "Not if you want to keep they fingers attached to your hands; not with all they hungry sharks swimming round."

He snatched his hand in and Terry fell about with mocking mirth. "It's all right, land-lubber," he said. "There isn't no sharks around 'ere, not that would bite your hand. You are so wet behind the ears, simple Jack. You stick your hand in if you want to. Nothing's going to take a bite out of you."

They sculled until they were adjacent to the headland and the whole of Tregenwyth was in view. It nestled into the hills and from out here, it looked so benign with the slate rooftops, half shadowed by trees, glinting in the sunlight. He avoided identifying his own house. He wanted to shut all of that out and just live for the moment.

At last, Terry laid down the oar.

"It's time to catch they mackerel, country boy," he said. "I hope you got the stomach for it; all they poor little fish with hooks stuck in their mouths."

Jack shrugged and sidled over to the basket, careful not to create too much imbalance in the boat's equilibrium. "I suppose they deserve it, old salt. If they didn't try to eat the feathers they'd get away scot-free."

Terry released the hooks from the cork rim and as each one was freed, he threw it into the swell. When the whole string had been cast, he handed the line to Jack. "You're learning," he said. "Now, just lift and lower that line gently above the water so the feathers look like they're moving."

He didn't have the line in his hand for long before Terry glanced over the side. "Take a look over," he said.

Jack leaned across. He could see darts of silver flashing under the surface. "Are they the feathers?"

"No. They're the mackerel what you caught. You can pull in now," Terry said.

He was excited and began to retrieve the line until the first fish appeared. Then Terry took it from him and carried on pulling until there were three mackerel darting on the hooks, their streamlined bodies flashing turquoise-silver as they twisted in the air.

"Grab!" Terry said, and Jack held the bottom of the line while Terry shook the fish onto the deck. For a moment he felt a twinge of distaste, but Terry was standing there, bronzed and beaming, pulling in more of the line and revealing yet more fish. It was the thrill of the hunt;

something Jack had never experienced. He watched as Terry swept the fish up, storing them in a basket and then throwing the line out again.

Soon he was even more pre-occupied with the fishing than Terry. He learned to cast, feeling the swell under him, watching the flecks of silver glint in the water as they heaved their catches onto the deck. He was captivated, but as they fished, the punt drifted westward.

By the time Terry noticed, they'd moved well beyond the headland and a whole new landscape was unfolding.

"The tide's took us," he said.

What they could see now was a rugged cliff with a cluster of trees clinging to the cliffside and rising green downland following its contours to a cove.

As soon as Jack saw it, all the dread of the house and that other Tregenwyth flooded back. He knew those woodlands and the cove, and he knew the path that meandered between them. It was part of the déjà vu again. His stomach lurched and he couldn't help himself. He let out a gasp and Terry laughed derisively.

"You really are a great land-lubber, man," he said. "We drifted on the tide a bit. But it isn't no sweat to scully back. It's no big deal."

Jack made a super-human effort and pulled himself away from the disorientation. "There are woods up there," he said, and he tried to sound as off-hand as he could. "Right up on the cliff edge."

"Yeah, Trelawny's Wood," said Terry. "That's where Batty Batten goes when he's on his trips. They do say they woods is haunted."

Hearing the word *Trelawny* sent more shock waves through Jack. He knew that name. The cove was significant too; but he couldn't pin down why, and something about that cliff path put a fear in him. Like everything else, none of these apprehensions made sense. To his certain knowledge, he had never been up on those cliffs.

He wanted to find out about the cove though, and he asked Terry.

"Three Corners' Cove?" Terry said. "It's dead quiet in there. Only locals know about it. And they don't go across they cliffs that often, what with it having the reputation for being haunted and everything."

"People really believe that?"

Terry grinned. "They're a superstitious lot down 'ere. People do say they seen this girl flashing between the trees dressed in a white shroud and she sings this weird song. It pretty near scares the daylights out of the locals."

Jack shuddered. The girl dressed in a white shroud…it had the same familiarity as all the rest.

"It's all right though, Three Corners' Cove," Terry said. "Little sun trap in there and lovely and quiet. I go in for a swim sometimes. We could do it now if you fancied – take our food in – then we could have a dip."

"I haven't got my swimming gear," said Jack.

Terry laughed. "You don't need none of that rubbish; not over 'ere. I told you, nobody comes down 'ere. You can strip off and swim, then dry in the sun."

"What – skinny-dipping?" said Jack.

"That's what I do, but if that bothers you, you can always keep your pants on. They'd dry out soon enough afterwards."

Jack stared at the cove. It wasn't exactly inviting. The cliff seemed to glower and there were swathes of dark shadow concealing the secrets of the whole coastline, but like Terry said, areas of gleaming sand were bathed in sunlight. He could see what a suntrap it would be and he was beginning to think, with Terry there, it would be a good time to spike some of his anxieties.

"Okay," he said. "We'll eat first and see how it goes. I might be up for a swim, as long as there's nobody around."

Terry began to scull towards the beach and the boat moved easily, carried by the inward roll of the waves. At last, there was a grinding as the hull slid onto the shingle and the punt shuddered to a halt. Terry threw off his trainers and clambered into the water, dragging the boat further up the beach, and Jack followed, pushing the stern until it was free of the waves.

"Tide isn't in yet," Terry said. He took a bottle and bag from the bow. "We'd better keep an eye on her. We don't want her drifting off."

They made their way up the beach and found a spot where the sun beat down from a cloudless sky. There was a cluster of rocks providing shelter and they settled, resting against the rocks. From where they sat, they had a clear view of the punt and the skeins of encroaching surf. There was no danger of the boat drifting off without their knowledge, and all around, the crucible of the cliffs rose with nesting gulls and kittiwakes swooping across from cliff to cliff. It should have been perfect and Jack tried desperately to recapture the warmth and contentment he'd felt when they were fishing, but although the waves lapped and the sun was baking, there was still a nagging contradiction that he couldn't resolve. Some layer in his head tainted everything around him with menace.

After they'd eaten, they sprawled out. Terry said they weren't going to fish anymore because, if they caught more, he wouldn't know what to do with them.

"Your da will want some, won't he?" he said.

Jack stretched his limbs in the sunlight, spreading fingers and toes. "Yeah. If we have two each fried up, that'll take six off your hands."

"He can have a few for the freezer as well if he likes," Terry said. "Mind, we can always sell what we don't want."

"Are you allowed?"

"No one never stopped me," Terry said. He sat up and looked across to the punt. The tide had been creeping further up the beach and now it was lapping the stern again. "We need to pull her in a bit more," he said. "Then I'm going to have a dip."

Jack took in the toppling waves and the glinting undulations out in the cove. It looked inviting. He thought total immersion might chill him out too, so after they'd dragged the punt out of harm's way, they stripped and plunged into the sea and soon the vitality of being in the water, the vigour of swimming, clambering onto rocks, diving, pitting themselves against each other as they powered across the cove, pushed the unease to the back of his head.

"You aren't bad for a country boy," Terry said as they turned at the other side of the inlet.

"It's a bit different, swimming here," said Jack. "Not like lengths in a heated pool."

"Which one would 'ee rather be doing?"

"This," said Jack without hesitation. "It's more like living, with the waves and being outside and the sun. There's no contest."

They rolled over onto their backs and eased across the bay again; but, as they powered through the water, Jack noticed a kind of reflection in the cove. It made him stop. He pointed it out to Terry, but Terry just laughed. "That'll be a bottle or something, a bit of glass. There isn't no one up there."

Jack rolled onto his front again and trod water. He tried to put the thought of another occupant out of his mind and they stayed in the sea for the best part of an hour.

When they got back to their clothes, the tide had already retreated, and for a while, they lay on the sand, letting the sun evaporate the moisture from their skins and all the time, Jack concentrated his mind on soaking up what should have been a perfect afternoon; but he couldn't do it.

There was that feeling of familiarity and also a sense in his head that the cove and these cliffs harboured a darker past, some brutality and villainy that he'd had some part in, and what was more, he couldn't get the idea out of his head that they weren't alone.

It was just a feeling at first, but as the wetness on his body dried to salt crystals and the warmth soaked through him, he became more certain. Something or someone was watching them. It was an eerie feeling. He couldn't be certain if it was a hangover from that time in his room yesterday or if it really was happening. He tried to ignore the premonition, but then he heard noises – shingle rubbing against shingle, as if something had moved further up the cove, and he sat up.

The sand lay littered with seaweed, and still the sun beat down. It created ripples of mirage across the cove. He couldn't see any sign of another body and he decided the noise must be a scuttling crab. He lay back again, but then there were more noises until it drove him back to sitting upright, and this time, he dragged on his trousers.

"What's up?" Terry asked.

"There's someone up in those rocks," he said.

Terry shook his head derisively. "You got problems, mister. You're just scared of being stripped off, that's all. I told you, no one ever comes out here."

"Well I'm going to have a look," said Jack.

Terry pulled on his trousers and followed with a resigned sigh. They clambered across the beach towards the spot where Jack had seen the glint of light, and as they neared, a stone spun across the sand bouncing on the shingle, coming to a halt at their feet. Then there were more and Jack whispered, "I told you. There's someone up there."

They approached more cautiously now, following the trajectory of the missiles, and as they rounded a rock, they saw a young guy – he must have been in his early twenties, perhaps younger. He was leaning against a boulder and he looked a mess. He had black, matted hair, hanging down to his shoulders, and his face was pale. When Jack saw him, he stopped and breathed in sharply.

There was dried blood around his face and his mouth had been cut. The right side of his face was shadowed in bruises, one on his cheek and the other half closing his eye. His arms were bare and scratched. He had a buff T-shirt on that was ripped across the right shoulder, revealing another livid bruise.

His legs were lacerated with scratches showing below his shorts. He looked at Jack and Terry and dropped a pebble from his hand. He didn't speak, but Jack ran across to him straightaway. "What's wrong mate?" he asked. He knelt down beside him, speaking as calmly as he could; but his mind was in turmoil. The first thought in his head was a picture of thugs on the headland armed with clubs and sticks on a dark night, and a sort of soldier boy being chased up the cliffside...but this kid wasn't a soldier. He looked more like a drop-out. "How long have you been here?" Jack asked. "Did you fall down the cliff or something?"

The guy shut his eyes, wincing slightly. "Something like that."

Jack looked at Terry. "Can we get him to the punt, do you think? Get him back to my place. Dad can contact Mum. Either she'll come home or she'll have an ambulance out for him."

"You'd best not move him," Terry said. "He might have broken something. Better to phone. I got my mobile in the punt."

"You won't get any signal," the injured boy said. He turned to Jack. His eyes were dark and he had a penetrating gaze. "Anyway, this hasn't got nothing to do with your mother. What is she, some kind of cop or something?"

"She's a doctor," Jack said. "She works in the hospital in Polgarthen."

The young guy closed his eyes. He looked sick. "You leave her out of it then," he said. "I don't want no doctors messing with me."

Jack looked at Terry again. He didn't know what to do, if the bloke was refusing to be treated.

"You in trouble with the police?" Terry said.

"That's none of your business."

"Have you broken any bones? Can you move?"

"Yeah, I'm fine." He eased himself into a more comfortable position, wincing slightly. "I've just picked up a few scrapes, that's all."

"We must be able to get somebody to help you," said Jack again.

The boy looked at him closely, as if he was weighing up whether he could be trusted. "You can get someone," he said at last. He pushed himself further up the rock so that he sat upright and Jack could see every movement jarring his bones. Then he dug into his pocket and pulled out a folded paper. "There's a bloke in Tregenwyth I need, like yesterday. If one of you can get this note to him...the quicker the better? Could you go over the headland? It wouldn't take so long that way. It doesn't take two of you to scull that boat back, does it?"

"No," Jack said. "I could go over the cliff." He was reacting in overdrive and his brain hadn't kept up. There was something about that cliff, and he'd never been up there before. He wasn't even sure he'd be able to find his way back to Tregenwyth. This seemed urgent though, and it would take at least an hour in the punt, possibly more.

Terry stared at him. "You be all right up there?"

Jack looked up at the banks of shale and granite. "Have to be, won't I? Who do you want me to give the note to?"

The guy moved again and his facial muscles twitched.

"Someone called Batten. Local choirmaster or something. Some of the locals call him Batty Batten. Do you know the guy?"

Jack heard Terry catch his breath and Jack was struggling to think straight.

"Yeah, I know him," he said, but suddenly, all enthusiasm for this mission evaporated. "He's my next door neighbour."

"What do you want with the likes of Batty Batten?" Terry asked.

The boy stared with his coal-black eyes and there was hostility in his voice. "That's my business. All you need do is get that note to him, like at the speed of light, okay?"

Jack noticed Terry's face harden. "If that's how you want it, I guess we can deliver the note, don't you, Jack?"

Jack nodded, but the prospect wasn't very attractive. They took the folded paper and made their way back down the beach and Terry could hardly contain his tongue. "I told you that Batten bloke was up to no good," he whispered. "I mean, look at the state of that guy up there. What's Batten got to do with the likes of him?"

"Do you think it's all right for me to take the note?" said Jack.

Terry glanced around him to be certain the injured boy couldn't hear, and lowered his voice. "The way I see it is this. We want to find out what Batten is up to, yeah? And this could be one hell of a step in the right direction."

Jack looked at the folded paper. Finding out what Batty Batten was up to sounded all right from the comfort of Tregenwyth harbour on a balmy summer's evening. But this was something else and it wasn't happening exactly the way he'd planned it. This way, for the next half an hour, he was going to be on the cliff alone, when, back in Tregenwyth, it had been his intention to pursue Batten along with Terry. Now, Terry would be out in the bay, bringing the boat back to the harbour, and the thought of crossing the cliff alone and then collaring Batten single-handed didn't make him feel at ease.

7

They went back to their things and Terry took Jack's holdall. "I'll put this in the punt," he said. "That'll leave you free for climbing the cliff."

"Is there a path?" said Jack.

"Yeah. But it's steep. Your bag is going to get in your way."

Jack looked at the cliff, but then he noticed the punt. Already, the tide had limped well down the beach, and the boat looked stranded. "We'll have to get that back into the water before I go," he said.

"I'll show 'ee the path when we've shifted 'er," said Terry. "You won't find it on your own."

They loaded the punt and dragged it over the shingle until its stern was in proximity with the waves again. It protested with every lurch, and as they struggled, a petulant voice came from behind the rocks. "Get a move on. It's like yesterday I want that guy over here."

Terry looked at Jack. " 'Ee don't exactly fill you with the feeling of good will, do 'ee?"

Jack was breathless. "No way," he said. "And it doesn't feel much like a mercy dash either. I mean, Batty Batten? If you were in trouble, is he the kind of guy you'd want to help you?"

"Not unless I was looking for a lethal dose," said Terry. "But I guess somebody's got to sort that bloke out."

With the punt poised at the water's edge, Jack followed Terry towards the cliffs. As they wound their way between the rocks, the heavy shadows of the rock face fell across them. The path climbed sheer out of the cove, shouldering between huge crevasses and when Jack saw it he felt stunned. It was like advanced mountaineering.

By now, the promontories of rock had hidden them from the injured boy's view and suddenly, Terry stopped. He looked around, thrusting a hand in Jack's direction. "Come on then," he whispered. "Let's have a look at that note before you go."

Jack unfolded the paper. It was a rough scrawl and there was a sinister brevity about it. *"I need you now. Greg,"* it said.

Terry breathed in sharply. "There's something going on around 'ere, mate," he said. "Batten and that bloke. And there's no way he fell down the cliff. They bruises didn't happen falling down no cliff. That guy's been in a fight."

Jack gazed at the escarpments, and now they were eerie with silence. Even the gulls had gone quiet. There were no screechings, no calls of kittiwakes and not a breath of air.

Something was very sour about all this and it chimed more with the nightmare of yesterday than it did with the reality of now. He shuddered. "It's weird," he said. "Who could have beaten the guy up? There's nobody out here."

They stared at the path as it forged its way through the chasms and then the querulous voice wafted around the rocks again. "Get a shift on. I want that guy Batten out here now."

Jack looked at Terry. "I'll see you down the harbour after I've given Batten the note," he said. "How long will you be?"

Terry glanced at his watch. "It's half three now. I should be back by quarter to five. You mind how you go over they cliffs though...and we'll sort the mackerel for your da when I get back."

As soon as Terry had disappeared, Jack realised how alone he was. There were still no sounds and the cove had suddenly lost the warmth of the swimming and the lounging in the sun. Now it was filled with something else.

Feeling his way on the rocks, he began climbing. He was cautious to a fault. Where springs gushed through the shale, the slime was lethal. There were roughly-hewn steps, but they were slippery, and he groped, shouldering between the crevasses, gripping tufts of grass for support. The effort drained his energy and his joints and muscles ached.

Eventually, he made it to the top and gasping for air, unsure of his bearings, he scanned the spectrum of cliffs from west to east. Then a sensation took over every atom of his body – a feeling of black horror. All anxieties about Greg down in the cove, and of Batten back in the village were swamped. The feeling that swept over him was intense. As he stood there, he knew this wasn't the first time he'd been on this cliff and the memory was tangible in its immediacy. He stared at the path meandering towards the middle distance and he listened to the on-shore breeze tugging at the grasses and he knew the pattern of the cliff. He knew the inlets along the coast and the cove down below him. He knew the scar of a ravine funnelling inland. And nothing about it made sense. Its memory seemed to be cloaked in a star-lit night. This was where the men had been wielding their clubs, and the soldier boy was struggling against their rain of blows. The power of his recall was overwhelming.

Suddenly, in blind panic, he tore across the cliff, oblivious to the cavernous drops and the eroding path. He leapt over ditches, powering himself between the trees of Trelawny's Wood. He raced down the hill and didn't stop until he'd reached the security of the quayside and the conglomeration of milling holidaymakers crowding the jetty.

Then he leaned against the railings and gasped for breath. His whole body was trembling, and for a long time, he didn't move. But at last, something more like calmness re-instated itself and with the aid of serious deep breathing, he began to work out the next step.

He would have to confront Batten. Greg needed attention and that meant he couldn't put it off. Before he'd come over the cliff, there was half an idea that he might follow the choirmaster to the cove, but that plan had been scotched by what had just happened.

He'd give Batten the note and leave it at that. Another day, when Terry was with him, they'd follow the guy; but that would have to wait.

He took the note from his pocket and read it again. It couldn't have been more brief. Then, taking a deep breath, he set off along the quay, and steeling himself, turned towards the hill. He concentrated on how he might confront the choirmaster. He would try to be disdainful. He wanted to hint that he knew the guy was into things and to communicate how much he despised him. There had to be some kind of shot across Batten's bow.

It was strange walking past his own house, and he didn't knock on Batten's door immediately. He stood, summoning his composure. Then he rammed the ornate brass knocker and waited.

He knew he was still breathing more heavily than was good for him, and he was tense, listening for footsteps.

But there was nothing. He knocked again and still nothing. After he'd knocked a third time, he heard a voice from the other side of the road.

"You looking for Batty?"

He turned to see an old woman standing on her doorstep.

"I've got a note for him," he said.

"'Ee isn't in, dear. 'Ee do go off to Polgarthen on Tuesdays, regular as clockwork, and as often as not 'ee don't come back. 'Ee got 'is choir practice that night, see. If you got a note for him, that's your best bet – seven o'clock down the church hall."

Jack wasn't sure how he felt about that. He was frustrated. He'd built himself up for this confrontation; but he was also relieved because the meeting had been averted. He felt slightly anxious for Greg too. Greg had wanted the note delivered straightaway and he needed some sort of medical attention. He was still not certain about going to the choir practice and alternatives were flashing through his mind.

"What time does he get back from choir?" he asked the old woman. "I could deliver it when he's back. I only live next door."

"I know, my dear. Moved in a couple of weeks ago, didn't you? But it's no good you waitin' up for him. 'Ee don't come back here from choir, not straight off. 'Ee go out somewhere and more often than not, it's the small hours before 'ee do get back here."

He thanked the old woman and meandered back down the hill, conscious that she was watching him. He didn't go into his own house, and that would give her something more to think about; but he had no wish to go back there yet, particularly after the milling he'd got on the cliff, and besides, he was never keen to be in his dad's company.

The sanctuary of the harbour was what he needed and he had to be there to meet Terry. There were things he had to tell him about Batten's late night escapades. What kept Batten out until the small hours, and where did he go?

The more Jack thought about it, the more convinced he was that something was up and he was certain now that the noises under the cellar were linked to Batten's activities. Possibly they were linked to Greg as well.

He went across to the harbour entrance. He had a good view of Terry crossing the bay from there. He could already see him standing in the stern of the punt, his brown arms manoeuvring the oar through the water, and as he watched, thoughts raced through his head.

It wasn't the end of the world that he hadn't delivered the note. Greg wasn't going to die, and really, Jack didn't feel any great obligation to him. He was a bit of a jerk, with his expectations and impatience, and there'd been no sign of any gratitude.

It did mean an enforced entry into the choir though, and he didn't relish that prospect.

Terry was making impressive progress. He'd already reached hailing distance and when Jack called, he waved. Within minutes, he was navigating the harbour entrance. "Get round to my moorings, can 'ee?" he shouted. "And take the rope. Did you give Batty the note?"

"I'll tell you when you're in," Jack said.

When Terry had secured the punt, Jack climbed on board.

"What did he make of it then?" Terry asked. He collected Jack's holdall and pushed it towards him.

"He wasn't there. The woman opposite said he goes to Polgarthen on Tuesdays, and when he gets back, he goes straight to choir…and…get this. She said he doesn't come back from choir till one or two in the morning."

"That don't surprise me," Terry said and then he laughed. "What nosey old bag told you all that lot?"

"Don't know. She's a little old lady, a bit like a witch, with straggly grey hair and she has this shawl wrapped around her shoulders."

"That'll be Gladys Miners. I'll tell you what, simple Jack. There isn't nothing about the goin's on in Tregenwyth that woman don't know." He lifted the basket of fish and balanced it on the steps. Then he went back to get his gear. "What you going to do with the note now?"

"I'll have to go to choir, won't I? Give it to him there."

"Best of luck with that, then," Terry said. They took the basket and clambered to the jetty. "How long do choir go on?"

"A couple of hours, I think," Jack said. There was a resigned despair in his voice. "Two hours of mental torture."

Terry laid a sympathetic hand on his shoulder. "Well, when you've given Batty the note, after you've been through your singin' torture, you come down here and I'll buy 'ee a bag of chips."

"That would be good," said Jack. They sorted the fish and Terry took a piece of string from his pocket, neatly threading it through the gills, bunching the mackerel. Then he presented six to Jack. "Give they to your da," he said. "They'll be 'andsome fried up for your tea. Does 'ee know how to gut a fish?"

Jack laughed. "There isn't anything in the world of culinary arts that my dad doesn't know about," he said.

"Strange guy, for a bloke, isn't 'ee?" Terry said.

Jack nodded. He wished it wasn't so. He'd like his dad to conform to the stereotype but that wasn't his father's style.

They took the remaining fish onto the jetty where the tourists were milling and Terry began his patter. "Fresh mackerel! 'Andsome for your tea. I can let 'ee have them a pound for two. Have I got any takers?"

He was a master and emptied the basket in no time. Then he pushed half the takings towards Jack. "Here. You done as much as me, catchin' they fish. Bit of pocket money."

But Jack shook his head. "It's your boat and your line. And you sculled us out there. It was fantastic for me. I don't want any money."

Terry grinned and shook his head. "Look, simple Jack, if you're going to do this on a regular basis, you got to have some of the takings."

Hearing him predict that this could be a regular happening made Jack feel very pleased. He liked Terry.

The guy was good company and it was great going out in the punt with him. "We'll sort out something," he said. "But you keep the money this time. I've got half a dozen mackerel. That's payment enough."

"Well, I'll get 'ee a bit of fish as well as the chips tonight," Terry said.

They returned the basket to the punt. When Jack got home with his mackerel, Dad was delighted.

In fact, Dad was in a reasonably good mood. He was glad of the fish and he was pleased that Jack had agreed to join the choir. He didn't probe about why he'd changed his mind, but when his mum got home, she did, and that was typical of her. When it suited her, she'd dig around like a ferret. He had to come up with some story about how he'd thought it through and he'd conceded they might be right. It was a chance to get to know some of the other kids in Tregenwyth, even if they were a bunch of 'Bible bashers'. But he was irritated by his mum. She could delve about his change of heart with the choir, but when it came to his dislike for the house, she didn't want to know.

He felt apprehensive as he set out for the village hall. He was painfully conscious of the fact that he wasn't that much of a mixer, and he found new situations tough. He also knew that tonight he was doing something very tricky. He was putting himself on a collision course with Batten. He didn't have any idea how it was going to pan out, and as he pushed through to the church hall, he had this feeling he was stepping into a minefield.

Batten was at the far end of the hall. He was with the guy who played the keyboard. They were shuffling through various scores. The other members of the choir were scattered in knots around a table, drinking tea or coffee. Some of the kids had soft drinks and a couple looked up as he came in. One of the older men came over.

"Can I help you?" he said. "Are you looking for someone?"

Jack nodded. "I've come to join up, haven't I? I need to see that guy, Batten, the choirmaster."

The old man looked pleased. "You're going to join us?" he said. "That's really good news. And you'll be especially welcome if you're a treble. You do sing treble?"

But Jack was itching to confront Batten. He hated all this small talk.

"I guess so. Is that Batten up there?" He moved away, heading down the hall, wanting the old man to go back to his tea and biscuits. "I'm going up to see him, okay? He knows I'm coming. My dad told him."

"He's busy at the moment with Mr James," the old man said.

"No problem. I'll hang around till he's done." He headed off before the old guy could say any more and he knew Batten was aware of him. But he didn't make any move to end his discussion with the keyboard man. All he did was wave a hand in Jack's direction — a curt instruction for him to stand and wait his turn.

Batten was a squat man and he had a very individual style of dress: smart creased trousers and black, well-polished shoes. He had a bright shirt, green, with a silk sheen about it and he wore a cravat. It was all very eccentric, but it was neat. He was bending over the keyboard, so none of his facial features were visible, but Jack was conscious of that mean streak in him. He made him wait an inordinately long time. It was almost as if he was making a point, and that rubbed Jack up the wrong way. He began to feel decidedly aggressive.

When Batten did finally deign to move his frame in his direction, the first thing Jack noticed was a stench of stale cigarettes and a pungent whiff of deodorant. It almost made him choke, and inadvertently, he stepped back. He looked more intently at the choirmaster.

He'd never really seen him at close quarters and confronting him now was chilling. He was peculiar in every way, with a flaccid hairless face and a complexion like raw pastry. He was balding, but there was hair around the back of his neck that was more like fluff. He'd attempted to cover the baldness, dragging strands of nicotine-yellowed hair across from a low parting, and his eyebrows were so pale, they were almost invisible.

Jack was conscious of the small, piercing eyes too, cold and venomous. His mouth twitched with irascibility as he approached. "You want me?" he snapped, and suddenly, a burning defiance welled up in Jack. He wasn't scared of this creep. He just wanted to wrong-foot him.

"Yeah, Mr Batten. You're the choirmaster, right? I'm your new neighbour. My dad told you I might be interested in joining the choir."

Batten stared straight through him, his eyes narrow and his tiny mouth still twitching. "Your dad?" he said. "Oh, the O'Hagan fellow you mean. Can you sing, boy?"

"I wouldn't be here if I couldn't," Jack said, but the disreputable old face, pushed in front of him, galvanised his distaste. "Well, that's not exactly true is it? Because me and my mate, Terry Blewett, we went fishing around by Three Corners' Cove this afternoon."

He watched Batten's face. He was looking for any change in his demeanour, and he did sense a flash of light in his eyes and the mean mouth twitched even more, but Batten didn't give much away. "I fail to see the connection," he snapped. "If you want to join the choir, give your name to Mr James and then get back there with the rest. If, on the other hand you're here just to bandy words about some fishing trip, then get out now."

But Jack didn't flinch. "The thing is Mr Batten, we beached for a bit and went ashore."

He wanted to string this out because it would make it easier to gauge Batten's expression. The guy wasn't quite so cool now either. "So you beached," he said. His facial muscles were twitching and his eyes were narrowing. "And why is beaching at Three Corners' Cove a reason to intrude on my valuable time?"

"There was a guy there," Jack said. "On the beach. Me and Terry found him. A young guy called Greg."

When he heard the name, 'Greg', Batten's tone changed and Jack saw his skin pallor colouring slightly.

"So, you saw a young guy ... and that gives you leave to commandeer my time?"

"The guy had been bashed about, Mr Batten, black eyes, bruises – cuts to the face and shoulder. He was in a bad way. We wanted to get him to a doctor."

By now Batten's eyes were darting around the room, but he persisted in maintaining his ignorance. "I'm still at a loss to see what it's got to do with me," he snapped.

"He told us he didn't want a doctor. He said he wanted you, the choirmaster, Mr Batten. He gave me a note for you."

A look of urgency suddenly flashed in Batten's eyes and he led Jack to a darkened corner of the hall. "Not so loud," he whispered. "Now, this Greg person, he was injured, you say?"

Jack nodded. "He said he fell, but it looked more like he'd been in a fight."

"And the note?" Batten looked around and held out a twitching hand.

Jack took the folded paper from his pocket, still watching the choirmaster's expression. He didn't hurry. He was certain that this guy was involved in something bad.

Batten snatched at the note and his eyes scanned the message. "When did you say you saw him?"

"This afternoon, about three o'clock."

Batten nodded. "Did he say anything else?"

"Nothing much. He didn't say much at all, really. Just, he didn't want a doctor or hospital. He gave me the note and he said he wanted you to get it, like yesterday."

Slowly, the expression on Batten's face returned to normal and he pocketed the piece of paper. "Strange fellow," he said. "I hardly know him, but not to worry, I'll deal with him. I'll see he's all right. Now..." he looked around again, "are you planning to join us or not? As a treble? Your dad was full of praise for the quality of your voice."

"May as well," Jack said. "Now that I'm here."

"I'll need more commitment than that," Batten snapped. "If you intend to join, I expect you to make it your top priority. Give your name to Mr James and then you can get a drink."

But Jack's mind was racing. The more he saw of Batten, the more he recoiled. The house seemed to have had a tortured past, but Batten was a big problem too. There was something innately evil about him and Jack felt he would have to tackle both situations. He couldn't carry on existing here with things as they were. He and Terry had to find out about the voices in the caves, and Greg, and Batty Batten...and being in the choir might help. Jack had already unsettled the guy.

Drifting groups of singers were gathering at the front now and he took his place with the trebles. Then Batten introduced him. "Gentlemen," he said. "We have a new member. A Mr O'Hagan. He will be joining the trebles and we trust his voice will add to the general timbre of our choir."

And Jack's voice did add to the general timbre. His mum was right; he had a very good voice and he'd been in school choirs since he was about eight. He found sight-reading easy and the music didn't present him with any difficulty, but, tonight, his singing was unnaturally good. His voice was stronger and fuller, and that unnerved him. And another thing was confusing him. At the back of his mind, he sensed someone telling him that he had the voice of an angel...and he couldn't escape the feeling that neither the voice nor the comment were part of him. There was the sense that all this was somehow linked to the experience he'd had in his bedroom, and he was beginning to think there was more to yesterday than he'd realised. The feeling was growing that, in some weird way, that moment of madness had messed with his brain.

All through the choir practice, the equilibrium was out of balance. This voice, Greg in the cove, things in his head that were coming from outside this world, the young soldier with the drawn sword, the men on the cliffs with clubs and Batty Batten, they all seemed to be merging into one huge morass.

By the end of choir he'd had enough. He was eager to get out of the church hall and back down to the relative sanity of the crowded jetty and Terry Blewett.

8

But Mr Batten had different ideas.

As the others began to disperse, his voice came across the hubbub with: "O'Hagan, you will stay back. I want a word with you before you go."

The trebles on either side of him nudged each other and exchanged winks, and there were heavily loaded grunts of "Uh-uh." The kids dug Jack in his ribs, but he responded, signalling his contempt and shoved his way out into the hall.

Batten's tone had not been designed to put him at ease and as the choir members jostled for the door, he had to steel himself in an attempt to re-kindle his earlier defiance.

The choirmaster was standing by his music stand shuffling scores and he didn't look up until the last of the others had gone. Then he crooked his finger and his eyes narrowed. There was that stench again. It surrounded the guy like an offensive aura.

"Now, boy," he said. He spoke in a low monotone, still shuffling his music, but with his gaze firmly on Jack, staring right through him, and the eyes that were glinting through those narrowed eyelids were flashing like lasers. "The youth at Three Corners' Cove."

"Yeah, what about him?"

"Just this." Jack could see the cold whites of his eyes, yellowed by years of nicotine addiction. "Forget about him. I'll sort him out." Then he added, in a voice that would have frozen ether: "And it would be in your interest to forget everything that passed between us tonight. You'd be well advised to keep away from those cliffs and the cove too. I've no doubts the youth did fall as he claimed. You see, boy, it's very treacherous up there, extremely dangerous." He was staring right into Jack's face now, his pasty features twitching, but those pig-like eyes were as still as ice. "I am telling you this, O'Hagan, for your own well-being, is that understood? I would hate what befell the boy in Three Corners' Cove to befall you and your friend. You do understand what I'm saying, don't you?"

Suddenly Jack was rigid. This was about as unveiled a threat as he'd ever heard, but he bit his lip in defiance.

"Yeah, right," he said. "But are you sure you don't want my mum to see this Greg guy? I mean, she is a medical registrar."

"I can manage," Batten snapped. "Now, you cut along…and remember what I've said. Steer clear of those cliffs and Three Corners' Cove. You've been warned."

Jack headed for the door. The adrenaline was racing through his veins, and as soon as he was clear of the hall, he ran, not stopping until he'd reached the sanctuary of the harbour.

Terry was perched on the quay wall and when he saw Jack, he chuckled. "That bad, was it?" he said, but Jack was in no mood for laughing. His heart was thumping and he could barely get a grip on his breath. All his earlier cockiness had evaporated.

"You've got no idea," he said, clambering up beside him. "That Batten guy is into bad, like...the bloke is totally evil."

"Why?" Terry's eyes burned with curiosity. He moved slightly to make room for Jack. "What happened?"

"There's something going on with him and that Greg guy. That's for certain. He pretended he hardly knew him, but he didn't want Mum to treat him, and he warned us off, no messing, like, he threatened us."

"How do you mean, threatened?"

"He as good as said if we didn't want to end up like Greg, we'd better steer clear of the cliffs and Three Corners' Cove."

Terry breathed in sharply. "He threatened to duff us up, you mean?"

"Not in so many words, but I knew what he was driving at...and he knew I knew. He tried to make out that Greg had fallen and that's what would happen to us if we carried on going up there."

Terry shook his head. "Greg didn't fall. That guy's been in a fight. I seen people in fights often enough and that's what Batten's threatenin' us with." He stopped then and drew breath, nudging Jack, nodding towards the quay road. "And 'ee's off up there again now, look."

Jack turned to see Batty Batten, pacing across the harbour head with a determined vigour, heading for the footpath and the cliff.

"Quick, down off the wall," Jack said. "I don't want the guy to see us."

They slid down to the quay and watched.

Batten was glancing around as he charged through the crowds, and there was that furtive look again, as if he was desperate to get to the cliffs unobserved.

"Are we going to follow him?" Terry whispered.

Jack shuddered. It was too soon after what had happened at the church hall, and his experiences on the cliff that afternoon had been so powerful, he just didn't have the stomach to face it all again.

"Not this time," he said. "He'll be looking out for us. It's at the front of his head we know he's going up there, and the guy's dangerous. If you heard the way he talked, I mean. He's lethal."

"Fair do's," Terry said. "We'll follow him another night. 'Ee's always going up there. We got plenty of chances."

Deep inside, Jack felt as if his fear was some kind of a failure. Terry was his mate though. He could be straight with him. "Sorry," he said. "But that guy scared the crap out of me tonight."

"It's okay." Terry put his hand in his pocket and drew out a fistful of change. "I promised 'ee fish and chips didn't I? You up for that?"

Jack nodded and smiled. He didn't think, in all his time in Stevenage, he'd had a mate who'd shown that kind of sensitivity. Terry knew Jack had chickened out; but rather than berate him, he'd just accepted it and steered him away, guiding him back to the normality of comfort food.

They had a tray of fish and chips each, and as they ambled along the quayside, his mood changed. They deliberately tormented the gulls, dodging their swooping forays which sent the birds wild with fury.

The lightness of the mood and the harbour antics effectively lowered Jack's guard and he was still chuckling as he began to climb towards the house, – and that was a mistake. The ambient change suddenly punched at him, and because he was unprepared, the impact was massive. The houses on the hill cast their brooding shadows on the ground and the dramatically darkening atmosphere closed in on him. Tonight was like it had been last night, only worse. The street seemed alive with sensation. The glowering buildings, the creeping shadows, the bilious glow from the streetlamps, and it all had a familiarity that was not of his time. In his mind, there were horses' hooves on cobbles and for a moment, the light of the streetlamps shivered away to cold moonlight. As he headed in the direction of the house, he could sense a presence, and in the vague flashes of the moonlight, there was a shadow, cast by someone following him, someone wearing a heavy cape, and there was the tapping of a cane on cobbles.

He speeded up, keen to get off the street. He was wrestling with his thoughts, trying to convince himself that this was all born out of his own imagination.

But by the time he reached the door of the house, there was a cold sweat on him. He was looking for some kind of sanctuary beyond the door, but inside, the instability was even worse. He could feel the sensations of yesterday morning all over again. It was as if the demons were erupting from the cracks in the walls, from between the ill-fitting floorboards and materialising along the staircase. The doors leading off the drunken levels brooded with menace and the whole sea of sensations was suffused with suffocating stillness. It seemed that the stonework was breathing threats with the motionless poise of a lion, waiting, watching, crouching, ready to strike.

Jack went through to the lounge where he found his mum and dad spread out in easy chairs and he couldn't believe how all these intimidations were lost on them. He couldn't understand how he could feel them so strongly while his parents were so totally chilled.

"How was it then, Jacky boy?" Dad said, glancing over the top of his book. "Get to know a few people, did you?"

"Not so as you'd notice," said Jack. "But I can live with that."

"Did you *try* to get to know people?" his mum said. "Friends aren't going to drop into your lap if you don't make some welcoming move. Did you talk to anyone?"

Jack slumped onto a settee. "I don't know why you've got this obsession with me making friends in the choir. I'm not bothered about making random friends and you don't force friendships by talking to people. If anybody's going to be your friend, it'll happen. Look at me and Terry? I didn't try to get to know him by making small talk."

His mother sighed. "Sometimes I despair for you, Jack O'Hagan," she said, and disappeared behind 'The Times' again, but Dad put his book down.

"How about a game of chess before bed?" he said.

Initially, it seemed a good idea. Jack hoped it would take his mind off other things, but the mood of the house was all-pervasive, and during the long minutes when his dad was encumbered with his next move, the menace took hold. To begin with, it was just the fog of silence, stifling him, as if the house was holding its breath. Then he heard horses' hooves outside the window and occasionally, a protesting neigh.

What made it worse was the knowledge that his parents couldn't hear any of it. They ploughed on through the evening without flinching. And Jack's mind was flooding. There was the ticking clock in the passage and now, creaking floorboards. Down the hill, cartwheels jangled and his brain was in an uncontrollable overdrive.

It was impossible to play a good game of chess. He missed all the traps his dad set for him and eventually Dad began to lose patience.

"Come on, Jack," he said as his bishop swooped on Jack's queen. "Have you the least idea where this game is going?"

"I can't concentrate," Jack said. "I'm packing it in." He pushed the board to one side. "I think I'd be best off in bed."

Dad swept the pieces into their box with a shrug. "It's the same with everything you do, old son," he snapped. "You don't have any staying power."

"Yeah, right," Jack said. "Whatever, Daddy dear."

His mum grunted from behind her paper and Dad said nothing. He just gave a resigned sigh and put the chess set back on its shelf below the table.

Jack looked at them, sitting there in a fog of middle-aged complacency, and then he shrugged and headed for his bedroom. But sleep was miles away. It was so humid. He opened his widow and lay staring at the puce glow filtering from the streetlamp and it wasn't long before he wished he'd left the window shut. What he heard wafting up from the street set his nerves jangling. There were distinct sounds of horses' hooves and trundling cartwheels. He heard angry cries of carters, all sounding from another age. Down in the hall, the persistent ticking of the non-existent clock continued and nothing about the house was right.

He tried to close his eyes, but his head was full of confused images – Greg lying injured on the beach, and Batty Batten striding out across the cliff. He'd be out there now and would still be there well into the night. What did he do out there? His head mingled that thought with the tormenting images of men crawling over the cliff wielding sticks and clubs, and the soldier boy, standing with his sword drawn. There was the tapping of the cane outside his window again, and he could see those long shadows cast by the man on the hill, with the dark cape. Then there was the neighing of horses and still the cartwheels rattled on the cobbled hill.

He sat up, throwing the duvet aside. He was hot.

He could see the old iron key lying on the cabinet by his bed and images of that floated into his thoughts as well. He picked it up and turned it over, while in his head, he saw the figure of a girl wandering through Trelawny's wood and there were snatches of song.

He threshed and tossed until his mum and dad came up the stairs.

Then there was darkness. The streetlight outside his window was extinguished and veiled hints of a new moon sent shallow reflections onto his window seat. Down in the passage, there was the constant ticking of the long-cased clock.

His eyelids were beginning to get heavy and slowly, they closed. But as they did, his bedroom door swung open.

There was a hint of light hovering in the doorway. In the hot throes of sleep, he tossed onto his back, thrusting out his arms.

The light was flickering, tentative, moving into the room. Its static-blue seemed to be searching for something. Skeins of the light crept across the floor like wisps on marshland. They shivered onto Jack's bedside cabinet, finding the key, sending methane-blue flames licking, dancing onto the key's surface.

Jack's hand moved again, restless, and his fingers sought out the cabinet. The blue light shuddered, and it was as if the key and the fingers had become terminals. Then the muscles in his arm contracted, and in one move, his hand closed on the key, while cartwheels rattled on the cobbles outside.

Silently, he slid from his bed, comatose in sleep, and headed for the door.

On the stairs he turned towards the attic, still sleeping, and the stairs groaned as he climbed.

The temperature in the house began to drop from its August humidity to the chill of autumn, and outside, a carter called loudly. Through the skylight, the moon grew until it was half-full. Its light was shining onto the attic door. Wrapped in sleep, Jack took the key and pushed it towards the door's surface.

Then it happened again.

As he shoved at the door, the resistance fought against him, and a plasma of force dragged him through, shredding his cells, ripping them apart and re-arranging them.

In a violent eruption, he was hurled onto a rough wooden bed and the door swung shut, while glints of the half moon shivered onto a brass sheet, the bronzed panel that Jax used as her mirror.

Startled, she turned, and the nightmare faded.

She'd dreamt about Barney again. He was lying at the foot of the cove where the galley had landed.

It was a week since she'd been out singing on the cliff, and she'd had the same dream every night. Sometimes she would be above her brother on the headland staring down at him, while, at other times, she was with him on the beach, crouching over him, looking at his unshaven face, watching the hollow eyes, seeing his legs drawn up as his body seized in a convulsion. And always the dream ended with her running across the headland her slow legs leading nowhere.

She turned over, heard the clock in the hall strike five and closed her eyes.

Her head was filled with a cloudy confusion. Something had happened to her while she'd been asleep, some interruption to her dream. She thought it was another of those fits, like the one she'd had in the master's dressing room last week. It was as if nothing was right in her thinking.

She thought about the fits as she lay there; two, last week and each of them with a different effect; the one in the master's dressing room had left her thoughts all out of joint. But then again, it might not have been the fit that caused her muddled thinking, not with Mr Trelawny making her learn that song and forcing her out onto the cliff in the white drape. Having to do that, would make anybody's thinking out of joint. The only reason why she felt it might have been the fit was that when she went to bed that night, she'd had another fit and afterwards, the odd feelings in her head were gone. Now they were back and that made her uneasy.

She didn't want to get out of bed. It was too early and too cold, but the clock had struck five downstairs and that meant her day must begin.

She shook her hair into loose spirals and dragged herself from her blanket. Then she pulled on her day clothes and crept onto the landing.

Cautiously, so as not to disturb Mrs Spargo or the master, she made her way down the stairs, past Mr Trelawny's bedroom, past the drawing room, across the hall and through the passage to the kitchen, where she struck a flint and lit a lamp.

Then she pushed open the door leading into the yard and went out.

It was bitterly cold out there. The darkness hadn't yet given way to dawn and she groped across the cobbles to the middle of the yard where she felt for the pump. She had to summon all her strength to work it. The handle was stiff and the motion heavy, but slowly, with its iron joints creaking, she managed to get a flow of water.

She filled the two buckets that were standing ready, and then she caught some of the water in her cupped hands, splashing it over her face. Its chill took her breath away.

Finally, with her face washed, she picked up the buckets and staggered back to the kitchen.

For a moment, her eyes struggled to adjust to the flickering lamplight.

She placed the buckets by the sink, and with her heart heavy, set about cleaning and lighting the range.

She hated it here, and the longer she stayed, the more she wanted to get away. What happened last week had filled her with fear and loathing. She'd seen people on the cliff chasing her brother, wielding weapons and baying for his blood, and now she had no way of finding out what had happened to him. She was terrified he might have been killed. She'd been summoned to Mr Trelawny's drawing room every day to meet more people. And that made matters very difficult between her and Mrs Spargo. Seeing her singled out by the master put the housekeeper into such a foul mood, there was no living with her.

"He's givin' you ideas above your station, callin' you in there all the time," she said. "What's he want with you anyway, so secretive and schemin'?"

But she had no more idea what was going on than Mrs Spargo, and she'd been threatened with a beating if she breathed a word about the cliffs and what had happened out there. That only made things worse. Her silence served to feed Mrs Spargo's rage, and to spite her, the housekeeper gave her extra chores. She made her scrub pots until her fingers bled. She made her re-lay fires, clean and re-clean the silver, and if any tears spilled out, all she would say was, "There. That'll learn you to suck up to your betters, you hussy."

When Jax had come back from the cliffs last week, she'd worked out a plan to get away from this house.

Every Tuesday, Mrs Spargo went to Polgarthen to the market, taking the carrier's cart.

Jax had calculated that if she could make things right with Mr Trelawny, he would allow her to go to Polgarthen too, and when she was there, she would give Mrs Spargo the slip and lose herself in the crowds.

Now, though, with the housekeeper being in such a mood all the time, she despaired of ever getting to Polgarthen.

Yesterday, Mr Trelawny had come out of the morning room and announced, "I'll be takin' a drap o' brandy with the Squire and Mr Baldwyn tomorrow, Mrs Spargo, and I'd be glad if you'd let the maid serve us."

That had made her so furious, Jax hardly dared breathe, and she spent all of yesterday trying to keep out of her way.

If only she could get to Polgarthen, she'd see boys from the Excise and perhaps they would tell her what had happened to Barney. They may even help her escape, but there would be no chance now – not with Mrs Spargo in such an evil mood.

9

Mr Trelawny was in his smoking jacket when she went to the drawing room later that day. He was standing with his back to the fire, rocking gently on his heels.

The Squire and Mr Baldwyn. were with him.

The Squire, like Mr Trelawny, was heavily built.

He was wearing a wig and he was more bronzed and windblown than Mr Trelawny. But both of them had an imposing bearing that scared her. As she came into the room, the Squire stared at her as if he was sizing up a prize animal at market.

She couldn't see Mr Baldwyn. He had his back to her; but when he did turn, she let out a gasp.

He had a pasty, hairless face and he was balding. There was a kind of fluff growing around the back of his neck. He wasn't wearing a wig, and he'd attempted to cover the baldness of his head, dragging strands of yellowing hair across from a low parting. His eyebrows were so pale, they were almost invisible.

She couldn't understand why he seemed so familiar even though this was the first time she'd met him.

Mr Trelawny must have heard her gasp, because he snapped, "Good Lord, child, what's wrong with you? You look like you've seen a ghost or somethin'." He shook his head and turned towards the Squire: "Penryn girl, moved down 'ere from Devon," he said. "No brains whatever!" Then he hobbled across to the bureau. "She can sing, though. Like an angel she is when she's singin'."

He beckoned for her to come across to him and then turned to the Squire and Mr Baldwyn. "Would you care to take a drap o' brandy with me, gentlemen?" he said.

The Squire nodded, and Mr Baldwyn let out a greedy chuckle that made Jax' flesh creep. She was ordered to decant the brandy and she served it while Mr Trelawny made his way back to the fireplace. He drew on his pipe and raised his glass. "Well now, to business. Here's to a successful run."

The others looked at each other. They seemed uncertain. They glanced at Jax and Mr Trelawny turned to Mr Baldwyn. "Would 'ee be anxious about discussin' such matters with the girl 'ere, Mr Baldwyn? You mustn't mind her. She won't make 'ead nor tail of what we're sayin'. But, if you've a mind to wait 'till she's done 'er singin', then, we must defer to you — your wisdom, sir and your knowledge. We must always defer to you. That's so, isn't it, Squire Polglaise?"

The Squire nodded, but he carried on staring, and that scared her.

"You're looking like a rabbit caught in a gun's sights, child," he said at last. "And I can't think why. Like Mr Trelawny said, we only want for you to sing."

"That song I learned you last week," said Mr Trelawny. He gave her the white cloak from the bureau. "Put this on, so we can see how you do look when you're out on they cliffs charmin' in our boats."

She shuffled into the shroud, heart pounding.

She had wanted all this to be behind her. The thought of staggering over the cliffs again – singing in the dark with those cut-throats hiding in the scrubland filled her with a despair so great she couldn't put it into words. But it seemed the Squire and Mr Trelawny had plans for her to do it again, and it wasn't difficult to remember the song. It had haunted her all week, along with memories of her brother struggling up the hill, fleeing for his life.

"Ow huv-kolon gwra dos," she sang. *"A ny glewydh y'n koos,*
an eos ow kana pur hweg?
A ny glewydh hy lev a woles a sev'
Y'n nansow ow kana mar deg."

It was like a recurring nightmare and as she sang, the desire to escape burned in her again. She knew the only way to do it was to get to the dragoons in Polgarthen and tell them what was happening.

It seemed that Mr Baldwyn's fears about discussing matters in front of her counted for nothing, for as she sang, they carried on talking.

Between phrases of the song, she could make out snatches of their conversation, and her mind raced. "Good route," she heard…"Start up rumours." …"Make a good ghost."… "Put shore men up there."… "With plenty of batmen this time."… "Cutter running in from France."… "Tomorrow night."

"Na fyll Betty ger, na vydh yn ahwer,
Dha gelorn y'n degav dhe'th vos," she sang.

But, however hard she tried, she couldn't understand a word they were saying. She only knew it was bad. There'd been a rabble on the cliff last week, and "shore men" and "batmen" were names for that rabble. They said there'd be more this time.

"Ogh, gas dhymmo kres my, y'n degav gans es,
Ke dhe gerdhes, ny vynnav vy mos."

When she'd finished the song for the third time, Mr Baldwyn held up his hand in a gesture that made her shudder. It seemed so familiar.

"Well sung, my dear. A voice like a bell," he said, and Mr Trelawny smiled. He turned to the Squire.

"That'll carry clear enough to charm in any Cutter, don't you think, Squire?"

All the time, the Squire was fumbling in his waistcoat pocket. "Most beautiful," he said. "It do make me wish I was a Cutter myself, to be charmed by such a voice." He was staring at her again with a half smile. Then he raised an arm, beckoning her and she cowered. He took the palm of her hand pressing something into it, and her whole body tensed; but it was just a coin, although he held on, pressing with his thumb, and he looked very closely into her eyes. "You don't know what this is, do you, girl?" he said.

She shook her head.

"'Tis half a sovereign, child. 'Tis for the singin' you done just now and for what you'll be doin' tomorrow night when you charm in our Cutter from France."

It wasn't the money that made the blood drain from her. It was the certainty that they were going to make her do this thing again, and her mind was racing. She clutched the coin and breathed deeply. She must get to the dragoons in Polgarthen and it was going to take every drop of courage she had. Blind terror was driving her. "If you please, sir," she said. "Mr Trelawny gave me a sovereign too, sir, last week after I'd sung on the cliffs. So now I've got a sovereign and I've got a half sovereign. I'm afeared of keeping all that money in the house, sir, even though Mr Trelawny do keep a safe house. I've heard tell there's a good Counting House in Polgarthen where I could put the money for safe keepin'."

Mr Baldwyn and Mr Trelawny let out guffaws of laughter and even the Squire smiled.

"Damn me, Mr Trelawny," Mr Baldwyn said. "You say she don't know what she's about, but she's as cunnin' as a fox, sir. We'll 'ave to watch her, or she'll be puttin' up as venturer for this lot."

"And in your own bank, too Squire," Mr Trelawny chuckled.

She wasn't sure what had made them laugh, but their reaction threw her into confusion. It was hard for her to carry on. But she had to. She just had to escape from this place before they made her walk those cliffs again.

"Mrs Spargo's goin' into the market later, sir," she said, and she could feel her body trembling. "She'll be goin' in the carrier's cart, and I was wonderin' if you'd tell her to take me with her. Then I could see my money's safe in the Bank in Polgarthen."

Mr Baldwyn was shaking with laughter. "Sharp as a whippet, Mr Trelawny," he said.

"Sharper than I gave her credit for, and that's for certain," said Mr Trelawny. He was laughing too. Then he tapped his pipe on the mantel shelf and said, "If you've a mind to go, cheel, I can't see no reason why you shouldn't. I'll 'ave a word with Mrs Spargo and then you can get that money put away good and safe."

It was such a relief, she hardly knew how to hide her feelings and she trembled as she handed the cloak back. All she wanted to do now was get out of the room before they could change their minds.

She felt as if she'd already escaped, but any euphoria was tinged with a bitter fear.

When she reached Polgarthen she'd learn the truth about Barney, and if her brother was dead, she didn't know how she would be able to contain her grief.

10

The main street in Polgarthen was seething with people and animals. There were stalls randomly scattered, crowding each side of the road and cattle being herded into pens. Pedlars mingled with clowns and performing animals in the square. An old ballad singer was wailing to an ancient lute, and a villainous looking man with one arm was forcing a chained bear to perform tricks.

Mrs Spargo had been furious with her for going to Mr Trelawny behind her back, and she'd threatened to give her a whipping that would teach her, her station once and for all.

She never spoke all the time they were on the carrier's cart. All she did was sit clasping her bag, her face set, and when they arrived in Polgarthen, she just said, "Well, now you're 'ere you can fend for yourself, girl. I'm not havin' you hangin' around with me, and if you aren't back for when the carrier's cart goes, we'll leave you behind."

But Jax wasn't concerned with Mrs Spargo's utterances, and as she had no intention of being there when the carrier's cart left, Mrs Spargo's threats were empty. Her head was filled with anxiety about her brother, and she was thinking about the dragoons, struggling to remember all the strange things she'd heard in the drawing room earlier – things she wanted to tell them.

But as she climbed down from the cart, she was stunned by the rampant chaos all around her – the street stalls and side shows, the milling throngs struggling with their purchases. There were farmers steering sheep and cattle, men clinging onto roped dogs. The dogs were straining at other dogs and baring their teeth. There were men and women pushing through with caged fowl, and the raging cacophony bewildered her.

At the bottom of the street, outside an alehouse, she made out a knot of soldiers and struggled through the crowd towards them; but as she got nearer, her pace slowed. She could see that most of them were drunk and they didn't look the sort of men she could approach with ease. She was shocked because when she did finally reach them, instead of being friendly like her brother, they seemed hostile and their drunken stupor was menacing.

For some time she held back, buffeted by the crowds, and her head reeled.

She hadn't expected this. There was no compassion, and for a sickening moment, she almost wished she was back in Tregenwyth.

Then a farmhand staggered from the pub doorway and grabbed her by the shoulder. He was stinking of liquor and he began pulling her towards him, calling her his wench. She struggled desperately. It confused her too, because, even now, the dragoons didn't come to her aid. They just laughed and jeered. Then, as she was wrestling, scratching and kicking, someone else snatched at her and everything seemed to swirl in a malaise. The boy who had snatched at her punched at the drunken farmhand; and they were fighting like bears.

But, suddenly, her heart leapt and she couldn't begin to measure the emotions that flooded through her. She realised who it was in this tussle with the farmhand. It was her brother, Barney.

He looked down at her, his face in a sweat and gasped, "Hell's teeth, Martha. What are you doin' in this thieves' hole?"

He aimed a kick at the felled farmer's boy and hurled such a string of abuse at him, it almost shocked her out of her delight. Her ma had better not find out he knew so many wicked words.

"I thought you was dead," she gasped. "I thought they'd murdered you."

He pulled away and stared. "Murdered me?" he said. "Why would you think anyone had murdered me?"

"Those men on the cliff last week."

She saw him take another step back. The confusion registering on his face was mingled with disbelief.

"So it *was* you up on they cliffs!" he exclaimed.

She nodded. "I had to. Mr Trelawny made me. He said I'd got to charm his boat in. I had to walk all night in those woods and I saw they men with their clubs chasing you. I've been worried sick all week they'd killed you."

Barney stared at her and his eyes were wide with amazement. "Never mind the men," he said. "They was no match for me, but ...Trelawny, you said? It was Trelawny what made you walk they cliffs?"

"Yes," she said. "To charm in his boat. But those people, with the clubs and the ponies and the men in the cove — what was happening down there, Barney?"

He glanced around the street and pulled her into a nearby alley. "We can't talk here, sis. There's people around this market who could recognise 'ee, and if it got back to Trelawny you was seen talkin' to a dragoon, 'ee'd kill 'ee for certain."

It was all coming at her at once, bewildering her, leaving her dazed. Mr Trelawny – killing her? She'd known all this was bad, but she had no idea it was that bad. She was so thankful she'd got away, and she followed Barney gratefully down towards a grassy bank at the back of the houses. It was quieter here and she felt more relaxed. Her brother was still alive and safe and he'd see she was all right.

When they were through the alley and away from the marauding crowds, she looked into his face. Quiffs of red hair curled from under his dragoon's helmet and his eyes were turquoise-green and pale. But they were sparkling with excitement. "Don't you know what this is all about?" he said.

She shook her head.

"Well, what did Trelawny say? Do you know if there's anybody in this with him?"

"Mr Baldwyn and the Squire were with him today," she said.

Barney breathed in sharply. "Squire Polglaise? Him what owns the Counting House?" he said.

She nodded.

"And Mr Baldwyn, the assize magistrate? Are they plannin' for you to charm in any more boats?"

"They were – tomorrow night," she said. "Why?"

"Are you *sure* it's tomorrow night?"

She nodded again. "They told me I've got to charm in a Cutter from France. What's goin' on down there, Barney?"

He didn't answer for a moment. He just took her by the shoulders and drew her to him so that she looked right into his eyes. Then he said, "Listen, Martha. Do you know what 'Free Traders' are?"

She shook her head.

"Free Traders? Smugglers? Come on. I know Penryn isn't the centre of the world, sis, and there wouldn't have been none of this goin' on in Holsworthy, but you must know what smuggling is."

"'Course I know what smuggling is," she said, pulling back. "Everybody knows what smuggling is, but..."

He smiled and sat down on the grass, patting a place beside him. "You didn't think the Squire and Mr Trelawny and the likes of Mr Baldwyn were the types to be runnin' contraband did you?" he said.

She shook her head again. Her brain was spinning. "Squire owns a bank. What would he want with smuggling?"

"It's the likes of Squire Polglaise and Trelawny that runs the business. Polglaise would be the venturer. He'd put up the money for the operation."

The word 'venturer' made her draw breath. "Mr Baldwyn said that this morning," she gasped. "When I asked to put my money in the Counting House, he said I'd be putting up as venturer next."

"What money?" asked Barney. He looked at her and frowned. "They aren't givin' you no money for doin' this, are they?"

She nodded. "Mr Trelawny gave me a sovereign last week, and the Squire, he gave me a half-sovereign this morning. I said I wanted to come 'ere to put it in the bank. It was the only way I could think for getting away from the place. I'm goin' to give Mrs Spargo the slip and go back to Penryn."

She could see Barney was hardly listening. There was a look of steely determination in his face, and she'd seen that look before. She'd known it ever since they were children and it made her nervous. "Never mind all that for the minute, Martha," he said. "I want for you to think. Did they say anything else? Anything that sounded strange?"

She frowned. Everything she'd heard had sounded strange. "I heard them talking about shore men and batmen," she said.

"That's all smugglers' talk," said Barney. "Shore men, they move the barrels, load them on the ponies and bring them to shore, and the batmen patrol the place. They're up there for when the likes of we turn up."

"They said something about a good route, too...and about ghosts."

Her brother picked up a twig and turned it absently in his hand. Then he tossed it into a stream running at their feet and said, "The smugglers' route, sis, is the track they use for bringing in the contraband...and 'ghosts' is what you are."

It made her start. She'd felt from the beginning that these things were bad, but...for a moment she just stared at the eddies roaming the stream. "What do you mean – ghost? I aren't no ghost. All I do is sing. It's to charm in the boat."

But Barney shook his head. "That's what Trelawny told you, but I know smugglers tricks, sis. Tell me what they said you was to do up there."

She told him about the dressing up and the strange song, and he sucked a long breath through his teeth.

"You aren't charming no cutter, girl," he said. "Trelawny's set you up for a ghost. That's what he've done. It's what they do. They get you to wander around in the dark, dressed up in white, singing songs; people start thinking the place is haunted. That way they keep away, leaving everything free for the tub carriers and shore men to move the contraband."

Still gazing at the stream, she twisted a piece of grass around her finger until the fingertip turned blue. It was all fitting into place, and the more she heard, the more frightened she became. "That's a wicked thing they're makin' me do," she whispered. "Playing a dead spirit. It's heathen." Suddenly, she stood up and stared down at her brother. "You've got to help me get out of there, Barney. You've got to help me get back to mother."

But her brother didn't speak and that made her even more anxious. He just sat watching the water duck and dive between the stones and the expression on his face sent a shudder right through her. "Listen, sis," he said at last. "Would you do a real brave thing for me? I want you to put your money in Squire Polgaise's bank like you said. And then ..." he paused and stood up, looking straight into her eyes. "Then I want for you to go back to Tregenwyth with that housekeeper woman."

She could hardly believe he'd said it. "If I go back, I'll get killed," she said. "I told you, Barney, I came 'ere to get away from that place. They're wicked people and they're makin' me do wicked things. I can't do those things any more, especially now I know what I'm doing. You can't make me go back."

"Sis, you've got to," Barney said. "If you don't go, they'll start searchin' for 'ee. You know too much, and they'll find 'ee, even if you go home to Penryn. Believe me, I know these people. I've had dealin's with them. You've got to carry on just like you did before. You've got to do what they say. You'll be all right. Me and the dragoons will see you don't come to no harm."

The stream dappled at her feet, and she watched despairingly. "The dragoons out there are as bad as Mr Trelawny," she said. "They got brains soused in liquor. If I go back, it'll be the end of me. I'll be part of what they're doing and I'll never get away."

"You'll be all right, sis," he said again. "We'll get you out, I promise. When I've told my supervisor tomorrow, we'll go out and we'll catch Trelawny and his men red-handed. Then we'll have them behind bars. But if you don't go back, they'll know something's up and as well as going out searching for you, chances are they'll give up on the whole operation."

It was hopeless trying to persuade him. She knew that from past battles. Once Barney had made up his mind, there was no shifting him.

They clambered back up the bank and he kissed her on the forehead. "You wait here while I slip out," he said. "Then, go to the Counting House, like you planned...and sis, be brave. You'll be all right. I'll see to that."

Being brave was a long way from her state of mind. She was almost paralysed by her own desperation. There'd be Mr Trelawny's men and the dragoons in pitch battle on the cliff and she'd be caught in the middle of it. She'd be killed for certain.

As she groped her way to bed later, she was in a deeper state of hopelessness than she'd ever been.

She'd been called to the library after supper and Mr Trelawny had given her a string of instructions for the following night. And now that she understood what was going on, it struck an even greater terror into her. She knew about the contraband now and she knew about the smugglers' route. She knew about shore men loading brandy barrels onto ponies. She knew about the batmen lurking in the undergrowth with their staves and cudgels, and she felt as though she was being carried along by some destructive stream of fate.

There'd be no future for her beyond tomorrow, she was certain of that, and she tossed miserably on her bed. Then, as she lay there, contemplating her last night on this earth, her brain was taken over by a roaring and the world seemed to retreat around her. It was that fit again. Matter was disintegrating into tiny fragments, and her body felt as if it was being plunged into eternity.

In a swirling maelstrom, she was flung into the passage and hurled against the panelled wall where she heard voices, distant at first, but then more distinct. "Jack...Jack." And the fragments began to reassemble.

Names and faces tumbled in her head. A woman's name came and went, a...Mrs Spargo...the housekeeper...and the name they were calling her was wrong...She was Martha Jax, not Jack...Jack was a boy's name.

Still the voices persisted, and then someone began slapping her around the face, trying to get the blood re-circulating. And the name came again..."Jack...Jack."

It was his mother, and from the chaos, order began to re-emerge.

11

He was outside the attic door at the top of the stairs, and it was as if dreams were fleeing from his head. He knew it was his mum who was kneeling over him and he was beginning to acknowledge that he was Jack...and yet, Jack had sounded so wrong a few seconds earlier, and there were other things that weren't right. Something glowing from the ceiling was blinding his eyes. It was as bright as the sun. Was it the sun shining through the skylight? It couldn't be. It was night time and the bright light wasn't coming from the skylight anyway. It was shining from the ceiling. But it was brighter than any candle he'd ever seen. It was so intense he had to shield his eyes.

"Jack," his mother said again. She was shouting and slapping his cheeks.

"Don't do that," he said. He took his arm away from his eyes and pushed her hand. "I'm not a punch bag."

"You fainted," said Mum.

He could see Dad's face peering from behind her, lined with concern. There was a softer look to his dad. "Are you all right, Jack, old boy?" he said. "What are you doing up here by the attic?"

But that was the question. He had no idea why he was up here. The last thing he could remember was struggling to get to sleep in his bed and as for the bright light...he realised now...it was an electric light bulb, yet he hadn't known that a few seconds ago. His head was in total chaos. Why was he thinking, only just now, in terms of candles and the sun?

The house was doing things to him, just as it had two days ago, but this time it was happening in the attic. He shuddered. That meant it wasn't just his bedroom that was possessed. Every room in the house must have its own demonic memory and in some way, he was the lightning conductor, drawing out the furies.

Mum looked harder into his face, and she was frowning. "Your body seemed to go into spasm then, Jack. Are you feeling feverish?"

He was lying splayed across the stairs and faces, lights, bodies were all bearing down on him. It made him feel vulnerable. He didn't like that and he pulled himself into a sitting position.

"I'm all right," he said. "I don't know how I got up here and I don't know how I came to be on the stairs. I'm just here, that's all. It's no big deal."

"Well you shouldn't be here," Mum snapped. She was in doctor-patient mode and that boded badly. "You're sure you're not feeling feverish? You're very hot. Have you been having headaches?"

He sighed and closed his eyes. "No, doctor, I told you that last time. I'm okay. I did a bit of sleepwalking. I tripped on the stairs more than like. They're lethal, those stairs, and when you're climbing them in your sleep, well, you're bound to trip up."

But his mother wasn't listening. She had his wrist and she was timing his pulse. He knew what he'd said about sleepwalking and falling wasn't how it had really happened; but there was no point in discussing that with his parents. None of it was happening to them. The venom stored up in these old walls was directed at him and only him. It was he who suffered the déjà vu. He was the only one who heard the groans and creaks and those other sounds. And these attacks…it was almost as though when they happened, the house's history was dragging him back. But when he struggled to recall what he'd seen back there, nothing came into his head. There really wasn't anything to tell his parents.

His mum continued with her clinical analysis and he looked beyond her to his dad who was standing behind her, motionless. His face was contorted with anxiety. There was a softness of compassion in his eyes and suddenly, Jack needed that. His dad was an old woman fussing around with his domestic precepts, but the softness, the beating heart, right now it was a comfort. He grinned up at his father.

"It's all right, Jacky boy," Dad said, bending over and ruffling his hair. "We'll get this sorted. You'll be as right as rain in no time."

Mum glanced towards him. "Have you phoned?" she asked. "His pulse is racing."

His dad nodded. "They're on their way."

Suddenly, Jack's suspicions were aroused and his body stiffened. "Who's on their way?" he demanded, and as he spoke, he opened his hand and the rusted key fell to the floor. He was shocked that he'd got that in his hand again and he hid it as quickly as he could. Whatever had drawn him out of his bedroom and landed him up here in the garret had apparently made him pick up the key from his bedside cabinet as well. He began to wonder whether the key might be a significant link to all this.

What made him leap up in outraged dismay though, was what his mother was saying.

"We've called an ambulance, Jack. There's something not right here and I'm having you in hospital for a few days to do some tests. I'm going to find out what's going on."

"That's crazy, Mum," he said. "I told you, it's sleepwalking. You can't put a guy in hospital for sleepwalking."

"There's more to it than that," Mum persisted. "You're running a temperature and your pulse is up. You're sweating and it's the second time in two days. Better to be safe than sorry."

He looked to his dad for support, but there was nothing in his face that indicated he was on Jack's side. "It's for the best, son," he said. "I'll go and get a few things packed for you. And the ambulance will be here in two shakes."

He saw little point in protesting. Mum had made up her mind and even a nuclear blow-out wouldn't shift her.

"I keep telling you I'm all right," he said. But she was already directing him back down the stairs. "This is all a load of fuss about nothing. I don't want to go to hospital."

But she just looked at him and sniffed. "Typical alpha-male behaviour, Jack," she said. "You're all the same; scared rigid if someone so much as mentions doctors or hospitals, anything medical that might mess with your precious macho image. You're going into hospital and we're going to get you right, whether you like it or not."

His stomach was boiling. He hated hospitals and he knew there was nothing any hospital could do for him.

"I'm not dying," he said, but by now, his mum was thrusting jeans and a T-shirt at him.

"No, you're not," she said. "And if it's all the same to you, I'd prefer you stayed that way."

He acknowledged the house's unquestioned capacity to dream up torments that were out of this world; but the kind of torture they devised for him when he got to hospital was almost as bad. What they had in their armoury would have broken the most resilient operative in any secret service.

As soon as he'd gone through triage, fast-tracked because Mum was senior registrar, he endured unremitting indignities. He was wired up to machines that read his brain patterns. He was subjected to the sight of medics staring at fizzing oscillations generated by his head, and he had to watch their dead-pan faces as they nodded and wrote down notes, never smiling, never easing away from the rigour of their probings. Then it was terminals on his chest and more pyrotechnics on different monitors; they shone lights in his eyes and gazed intimately into his soul, they tapped his chest and back, they checked his reflexes with wooden mallets, they pushed un-warmed stethoscopes across him, listening with terrifying concentration to the beats of his heart. They wheeled him down long strip-lit corridors, they made him cough, they took blood, they took urine, and most of all, they took notes: long, copious notes about anything and everything, and all the time, none of their faces cracked into a smile.

His brain was in trauma. And it didn't stop until his inquisitors had done with him. At which point, he was dumped in a ward to navigate himself towards sleep, surrounded by heaving lumps of other disposed-of bodies, all of whom spent the dark hours moaning and groaning their way through to breakfast.

He hardly slept, and all night his brain wrestled with images of faces, gazing eyes, flashing lights, miles of meandering corridors, lifts, monitors, wires, terminals ... and a house back in Tregenwyth, shrouded in darkness, where time wobbled, throwing him from a venomous present to a rampaging past and back again.

The next evening, Terry came to visit.

By then, most of his tormentors had given up; but it had been a day from hell. There'd been a steady trickle of young doctors looking him over, taking more blood. They'd gone off with little vials of urine, although, why they should have been so obsessed with his pee baffled him completely. They kept gripping his wrist to take his pulse, and it seemed that a prerequisite to this heart monitoring was the intimate eye-stare. These guys and the young women who came to disrupt his search for inner peace, were mesmerised by his eyes. They stared into them as if they were probing the deepest of troubled waters, and always, there was this sincere expression on their faces, and they never uttered a word about what they were doing.

Occasionally, he was wheeled off to some new horror chamber to endure the probings of other monster machines with more demented waves on monitors.

Mum came in a couple of times, and when she turned up, she grabbed the wad of notes positioned at the foot of his bed and scanned them with the same expressionless face. It looked as though crossing the threshold of the hospital reduced all its practitioners to zombies.

"What's going on, Mum?" he asked. "I've been donating pee like it was some sort of currency, and I haven't any blood left."

She gave a half-smile and shook her head. "They haven't found anything," she said.

"Well, they won't, will they? All I did was sleepwalk."

But Mum just gave her superior 'I-know-best' look and said, "Let the professionals decide, Jack." Then she was gone.

The probings into his bodily functions were wearing him down, but the moments of inactivity, when there weren't any medical tormentors, were even worse. He was stuck in bed, and he was only allowed to get out to go to the toilet, which he did in secret for fear he'd have to donate what he produced to their ongoing investigations. In his ward, he was surrounded by other occupants – mainly old people who spent their time with their standard-issue blankets pulled up to their necks, just gazing at the ceiling or else they sat by their beds, still wrapped in blankets, and they didn't change their occupation. They still stared into space. When they weren't doing this, they were off to their mates on the opposite side of the ward, so they could regale each other with the most grizzly details of their operations.

All he could do was lie there and contemplate his awful fate.

He tried listening to the radio. There were earphones hanging by the bed, but that made his head ache, and he was impatient to be free.

There was nothing wrong with him except what the house was throwing at him, and whenever the medics left him alone, it was the house that filled his head.

Until he'd arrived in Tregenwyth, there'd been nothing to compare with what was going on back there. He had to admit he'd experienced the odd déjà vu moment and the shudder when people said someone was walking over his grave, but he was a realist and he'd always dismissed that kind of thing as mindless superstition born out of hundreds of years of unremitting propaganda about God and the after-life.

Jack's philosophy was simple. Time had always been the present and the population of the world consisted of those who lived in it at the moment. As time marched on, new lives came and old ones went; but that was it. No mystery, no spectral shadows left by the deceased; '*time past*' was '*time gone*' and '*time future*' was '*time yet to come*'. None of it existed in the present and the only thing that did exist was '*now*'.

But the house had rocked all that. Cobbled streets? The clattering of horses' hooves? The shadows of men in greatcoats from another age? The clock ticking in the hall? The feeling of instability where time didn't seem to be the steady marker of the present in any way? And these blackouts, where he came around confused and steeped in sensations of a by-gone age – none of it fitted with his pattern of thinking, and lying there, unable to block the thoughts in his head was bad. It was driving him down to the depths.

By the time Terry came, he was desperate for something to take his mind away from it.

Terry had a screwed up paper bag in his hand which he thrust in front of Jack. "What you been up to, then?" he said, grabbing a chair.

Jack took the bag and delved inside. It felt suspiciously light. "Nothing. I went sleepwalking last night and slipped on the stairs. The next thing I knew, Mum had me in hospital being grilled and probed by every medical freak from here to Plymouth."

"They got you in 'ere for sleepwalking?" Terry said. "Your ma's a nutter, mate."

Jack nodded. "Tell me about it. She's totally crazy." He withdrew a tangled mass of naked stalks from the bag and stared at Terry.

"Ate a few on the bus, didn't I?" Terry said, grinning. "Nothing else to do. And I wasn't sure you liked grapes."

"Well, you won't find out now, will you?" Jack said. "Not since your thieving hands have stripped the whole bunch bare. It looks as if it's been attacked by locusts."

"I reckon you'll find a couple if you search hard enough," Terry said. "Anyway, you're in 'ere under false pretences. You don't deserve no grapes."

"How come you knew I was in here, anyway?" asked Jack.

"You're da told me. I went up to your place to see if you wanted to come out in the punt. I tried your mobile, but it was off."

"I bet you still went, even though you should have been eaten up with grief because I was languishing in this dump."

"Yeah, right," Terry laughed. "It was a nice day and it seemed a pity to waste it. Did a bit of featherin' off Three Corners' Cove. Thought that Greg guy might still be there."

"Was he?"

Terry shook his head. "No, he was well gone."

"Baldwyn must have seen to him last night. I'd like to know what went on between those two," Jack said.

"Who the hell is Baldwyn?"

"You know very well who Baldwyn is. The choirmaster guy, the one we saw legging it over the cliffs last night, the villain who hinted that if we happened to take a trip up to Three Corners' Cove, we might find ourselves on the rocks with our necks broken."

"I know who did all that," Terry said. "That was Batty Batten, not some guy called Baldwyn."

Suddenly, Jack felt the colour rise in his face. Of course it was Batten ... but he'd said 'Baldwyn', and that name seemed to have etched itself into his brain from somewhere. He shuddered, because something inside him made him think it hadn't been a slip of the tongue. He could picture the man; only, the way he was remembering him now, Batten wasn't dressed in his normal clothes, he was dressed in a kind of Jodhpur trousers and mustard waistcoat and he was wearing a formal jacket, something out of another age.

He skated over it as best he could; there was no way he could explain it to Terry. "I meant Batten," he said. "I don't know where 'Baldwyn' came from. I don't even know anyone called Baldwyn. It must be all the grief they've given me in this hell-hole. I tell you, no way do you want to be brought in here, mate, not even if your life depended on it. I've been wired up to every machine in the place, and there isn't a square centimetre of my body that hasn't been probed."

Terry grinned. "Thanks for the warning. I'll bear it in mind." He settled himself in his chair and reached for the cluster of ransacked stalks, but Jack snatched them out of his grasp.

"Not likely," he said. "What's left in there is mine. You brought them for me and you've already wolfed most of them."

"Fair do's," said Terry.

Jack probed the stalks to locate one of the lone remaining grapes and he could see his mate was settling himself for a serious piece of chat.

"Last night, did Batten claim he hardly knew this guy, Greg?" he asked.

Jack nodded and offered him one of the remaining two grapes. "Yeah, that's what he told me."

Terry shook his head. "That's a load of rubbish. When I got back from fishing, this afternoon, he was there with this Greg guy outside 'Waves' – you know, the coffee and ice cream place by the pub? They was at one of the tables with their drinks, and their heads was stuck together like they was having a right old gas. There's no way Batten don't know the guy. I watched from the punt and they got up after a bit and headed off for the cliff together. They were dead set on something, and Batten was doing his usual looking-over-his-shoulder thing and he looked as guilty as hell."

"You reckon Greg's in all this with him then?" Jack said.

Terry nodded. "Come to think of it, that isn't the first time I've seen them together down the harbour."

"So, how come Greg got bashed up?"

Terry shrugged. "Search me. But I don't believe that had anything to do with Batten."

"If they let me out tomorrow, should we follow them, see what's going on?"

Terry bit into his grape. "Think you'll be fit by then?"

"I keep telling you there isn't anything wrong with me. I went sleepwalking. When they've got that through their thick heads, they'll let me out and I'll be fine."

Terry sat for a minute, playing with the stalk of the grape. "Are you sure you want to do this?" he said. "I mean, we could leave the guy to get on with it. He isn't exactly doin' nothin' to harm us."

Jack put the cluster of stalks on his bedside cabinet and settled himself more comfortably. "I don't like the guy," he said. "I've been catapulted into his choir. I've got to live next door to him. I reckon he's up to something down under our cellar, using the caves. I think he's a devious piece of filth, and somehow, he's managing to make the atmosphere around our place really bad. I want to find out what he's up to, and I want to stop him – that's if you're up for it."

"I'm up for it. I mean, it's something to liven up the day, isn't it – harassing Batten? I'll get a bit of a kick out of doing that."

Jack laughed. "As long as the kick isn't for real – something off of Batten's boot."

"He isn't no match for me," said Terry. "If you aren't out in time to do a bit of fishing tomorrow afternoon, we'll meet up after tea, down the harbour. You can text me or phone me."

They chatted about other things after that, the punt, the fishing, places to swim, what entertainment there was around Tregenwyth, the local female population, but all the time, there was a disturbing undercurrent disrupting Jack's thoughts.

He'd said that Batten was souring the atmosphere around the place …and he was beginning to think that was the truth of it. He'd called the guy 'Baldwyn' and he could picture him in those clothes from way back. The implications of that were out of this world. He was already coming to suspect that the two blackouts in the house had linked him with some kind of a past and his instincts told him that this past was bad. And now, what made all this so mind-blowingly unnerving was Batten. Batten seemed to be in both times. Was that right? Was he back there as well as being here? Was he some guy called Baldwyn back there?

When Terry had gone, his head was full of uncertainties. If Batten had been around in the other time as well and he'd been a force for evil then, it meant the guy was a kind of creature that could break the barriers of time and there was no way he was a normal human being.

The thought messed with his brain like an obsession. If Batten *was* in both times, he was some sort of evil time-traveller, and Jack didn't believe in time travellers.

It would certainly mean that he was the cause of all the disruption and that kept Jack's brain active all night. Until he got rid of Batten, the disruption would never stop. He couldn't understand why he was the only one to be affected by it either. Why not his mum and dad?

Any answer to that question was impossible to take in, because it implied that he was linked to Batten in a way that no one else was, and the link wouldn't be natural. There was some subliminal force binding them and that was too awful for his brain to contemplate.

12

Around ten o'clock the next morning, there was some frenetic activity directed at the bed next to Jack's. The old guy who'd occupied it for the best part of the previous day had been removed to some other place for the furtherance of his stagnation and now the nurses were remaking the bed. But there was an urgency about the activity which made Jack curious. There were whispers and knowing nods from the staff. He caught fragments of their discussion and that teased his curiosity. "Out on the cliffs," he heard, and "roughing it." "Young lad – couldn't be much more than twenty." "No knowing who he is – no name – no identification." And already, he was adding up the figures.

Then a posse of medics wheeled a shape into the ward, sculpted in blankets, attached to drips and oxygen and every other piece of paraphernalia imaginable. They formed a phalanx, shielding any view Jack might have, but whoever had been brought in was in a serious condition with capital letters. As soon as the trolley was adjacent to the neighbouring bed, they drew the curtains, obliterating all view, and for the next twenty minutes, there was a tantalising bustle of activity and whisperings. By the time the nurses and doctors had trooped away, he was at bursting point.

Mum was last out and he caught her eye.

"What's going on?" he demanded.

"Some kid," she said. "Brought in from the cliffs, been in a fight or something."

"Who brought him in?"

"The Culdrose helicopter noticed him on a beach during one of its patrols."

"Do you know who he is?"

His mum shook her head. "Some kind of homeless kid by the look of him. He'll be all right though. We'll sort him. Why are you so interested?"

Jack shrugged. "Bored out of my head aren't I? This is the only bit of excitement I've had since I've been here."

Mum gave a sardonic smile. "Well, we're discharging you. And I'll have a word with Dad if you've had a surfeit of boredom. I'm sure he can find an antidote. He's on his way."

The news of his imminent discharge was a relief to Jack. It meant he'd be able to go fishing with Terry that afternoon.

"Did you find anything wrong with me?" he asked, and his mum shook her head. She smiled again.

"Nope! According to all the tests you're A one – disgustingly healthy."

"I told you so," he said. "Sleepwalking – there was no need to drag me in here in the first place."

"Better safe than sorry," she said. "I suggest you get dressed so you're ready for a swift exit when Dad comes. Your clothes are in your bedside locker."

She stomped off and Jack's head was racing. He was really glad to be getting out.

But…he was going back to Tregenwyth – back to Batty Batten – and the house. The stress of hospital had dulled his memory about the house. Now, though, it had been confirmed that none of what was happening to him was caused by a malfunctioning body or a malfunctioning brain. It meant it was down to the house and he was heading straight back to it…and there was this person that had been wheeled in, too…

He glanced around the ward. All the nurses seemed to be on a coffee-break, and his fellow inmates were at the third level of stupefaction, gazing skyward, oblivious to what was going on, so he slid from his bed and darted across to the curtained cubicle. After a hasty look around to verify no one had seen him, he pushed through. And immediately, his suspicions were confirmed.

The boy lying there was Greg, and he was looking like death. His head and jaw were bandaged and he was so pale it looked as if there was no blood left in him. There were a lot more bruises on him – on his face, on the one arm that lay prone across the bed cover. The other was in plaster. And there were drips and feeding tubes attached to his body. There was a heart monitor and oxygen canisters, and Jack couldn't discern any movement. The only indication that he was alive came from a spasmodic convulsion flashing across the heart monitor.

Someone had really roughed him up this time, and the only living person who Jack associated him with was Batten.

His gut told him though, that there had to be others.

Batten was an intimidating guy and he gave off the general aura of menace and malice, but he was old and flabby. Someone else had to have done this to Greg – probably more than one person. Greg was too young and too fit to have sustained this kind of damage from just one person.

He stared at the prone body and shuddered. This was as near death as he'd ever seen.

He crept from behind the curtained cubicle and sat on his bed. What he'd seen had shaken him and it was a good few minutes before he could set about putting his clothes on.

Then he went straight outside to text Terry and the fresh air lifted his spirits slightly.

After texting, he went inside again. He knew Dad's capacity to cope with any kind of uncertainty beyond the domestic was flaky and he'd be in a serious state of angst if he arrived and found that Jack wasn't there.

But his dad didn't turn up for ages and that left Jack thinking about Greg. He couldn't believe the state he was in, and his mind baulked at what must have been going on up on that cliff.

When his dad did arrive, he deposited himself on Jack's bed.

"Sorry, son," he said. "Holiday traffic. You know how it is down here this time of year."

"No probs," said Jack. "But, can we go now, or do I have to be debriefed, get my parole papers or something?"

Dad laughed. "With your mother as chief warden signing your release, you mean? It's all done and dusted. You can get up and walk out of here without let or hindrance – as free as a bird and with not one blemish on your character."

"Let's go then," he said.

But almost as soon as the car pulled onto the road, things began to happen.

There was a strange contortion in what he saw. As they sped towards Tregenwyth, the scrubby hedgerows and the rolling hills with their rashes of trees and the counterpane of fields seemed too familiar, just as it was with the house and the cliff up by Three Corners' Cove. And in Jack's mind, he wasn't in the world of cars and tarmac roads. He was seeing hedges that were crowding in on him, almost scraping the sides of the car, and the road he saw was rough, rutted and pot-holed, more like a country lane. He felt the journey he was undertaking wasn't in a car either. It was accompanied by the clatter of horses' hooves and the rattle of cartwheels, and a cold breeze brushed his face. The trees he saw were wind-blasted and rusting to the colour of autumn; and it seemed that the instability was spreading. First it had been the house and harbour. Then it moved to the cliffs out towards Three Corners' Cove and now it embraced the whole of the land from Tregenwyth to Polgarthen...and it was swallowing him up. There was no respite and he gripped his fist firmly to calm his jangling nerves.

As the car headed on, he made a decision. Something had to be done about this. He couldn't just allow himself to get sucked under by these currents. Time seemed to be taking him like driftwood, buffeting him at will and if he just let it happen, he'd be bashed to pieces. He had to get some kind of a hold on things. He had to have, at least, some control over what was happening.

He thought about what he already knew and decided he would stand more chance if he collated it. He knew, for instance, that when these things happened, he was thrust into some sort of past and he was sure he experienced something back there, even though he could never remember what had gone on. There were hints though, and there was a guy back there who, in the twenty-first century, was Batty Batten; only he had another name – possibly Baldwyn. If, next time he went back, he could recognise him and make the link…and there were other things. It was almost as if the impressions that stayed with him could be dated to around the eighteenth century. There was a young soldier and rough thugs on the cliff wielding staves and clubs, and there was something bad going on, powered, he suspected, by Batten.

If he could remember all this, then perhaps he'd begin to piece together what was happening back there. There was a ticking clock in the hall and the name, Trelawny – that had a ring to it. The name had seemed familiar when Terry had mentioned Trelawny's Wood. Perhaps there was a guy back there called Trelawny.

They drove on and their progress became spasmodic. There were long periods of immobility as the beach-bound traffic ground to a halt. And all the time, he could hear the hooves of horses clipping the stones of a rough country path and there were cartwheels rattling across ruts and potholes.

He set his mouth as the cars ahead of them began to crawl forward once more.

Next time the forces took over, he mustn't allow himself to be overpowered. He must try to remember the actual events that were playing out back there. Then, whatever evil the house was harbouring would be clearer in his head. If that happened, he thought, he might just about hang on to his sanity, and with his knowledge, he and Terry could do something about Batten.

The nearer they got to Tregenwyth, the more he steeled himself but, when he clambered up the steps into the house, his resolve was shaken to its core.

Either he'd forgotten how bad the house was or something about the constancy of time had snapped while he'd been away. This time, he actually saw a long-cased clock in the passage. It was only a momentary vision, but as that faded, the shredded wallpaper where Dad had started work on the redecoration, dissolved into oak panels. And all around him, the walls were wavering as if they were caught in some kind of time warp. He glimpsed a candelabra hanging from the ceiling, and then it was gone. The light seemed to be fluctuating from day to night and as he stood there, he could hear the horses of another age stamping and whinnying outside. There was a curse from the kitchen and the sound of pots clashing and the whole place seemed to be on the cusp of breakdown.

For a moment, he just stood there, blown away by what was happening, and he put a hand out towards the wall to steady himself.

His dad grabbed him and said: "Are you all right, Jack, old son?"

He shook the confusion from his head. "Yeah, I'm okay. No worries. I guess I've been lying around too much. It must have upset my balance."

He bent down to pick up his case.

He had to be in control.

It was clear from the mayhem all around that a journey into the past was imminent, and in order to have control, he needed to be calm – grab tenaciously to the present, cling to normality. "I'll take my case up, all right?" he said. "I'll even unpack and stash the things in the right drawers. How would that be?"

His dad's eyes nearly popped, but being his dad, he still had to get his little jibe in. "Not the dirty stuff," he said.

"That goes in a device we call a washing machine. Being a boy of thirteen, you won't have any concept of washing machines, but they do exist, believe me."

"That's not funny," Jack said. "I'll bring the dirty clothes down and then I'll give you a hand with getting lunch."

He knew it was out of character and he said it, partly to knock his dad off his pedestal, and it worked. The incredulity on his father's face nearly made him laugh. But this trait of helping with domestic chores was something he'd noticed ever since the madness had begun. He was finding the thought of domesticity less irksome.

"I do need a few things down the village," Dad said.

But that was no good.

He had to be in the house. That's where his trips were launched from, and with his new determination to get a grip on things, he was almost eager for it to happen so he could find out more.

"I'll tell you what," he said. "You do the shopping and I'll do whatever needs doing here. Are we getting lunch or dinner?"

His dad's face was a picture.

"Are you sure?" he said. "I mean, normally, you need a manual to boil a kettle."

"You name it, son, I'll play it," Jack said and his father chuckled.

"Okay then, it'll be dinner I think. Boeuf Bourguignon, with Egg and Cheese Cocotte for starters and a nice Strawberry Pavlova to finish off. How does that sound?"

Jack grinned. "The strawberry season's over. I'll peel the spuds."

"Well, that'll do for a start," Dad said. He was almost bouncing at the apparent transformation. "But, just a small reminder, Jacky boy, it's the peeled potatoes you keep, not the peelings. You have got that, haven't you?"

Jack aimed a kick at him as he went upstairs. But, in spite of the banter, he was constantly aware of the forces rampant all around him. In his room, as he unpacked, there was a sensation of imminence, but...nothing happened, and it was the stifling silence that got to him.

It seemed that the focus for the disruption was downstairs. He'd seen the long-cased clock. It was at the end of the passage by the front door, and his eyes had caught glimpses of the oak panels through the scarred walls. But there'd been a kind of silence even down there. All the transformations had happened with an unearthly stillness and the noises he did hear seemed woven into the silence. They were outside the sphere of normality as if they weren't actually part of the world. Time was hovering and in its suspension, sound had been repressed.

He could still hear the tick of the long-cased clock. That was a constant, and from downstairs, he could make out more shouts from the kitchen, along with clashing pots. Outside, there was the occasional cry and the sounds of a street far removed from the world he knew. But none of this imposed on the silence.

As he heard the front door click and his dad leave for the shops, he suddenly felt alone.

But he had to be ready. He knew so much of what to expect. He knew where the clock was. He'd seen the oak panels in the hall and passage; he knew he'd meet Batty Batten, probably under the guise of some person called 'Baldwyn'. He knew of the cobbled street and the carters with their horses and their cries, and he suspected there was some character around by the name of Trelawny. With this much already in his head, this time it wouldn't be so traumatic, and being ready, he'd be in a state of mind where he could remember more.

He picked up the key. He knew something about that too. Although he had no idea why, the key was always there. It was a vital part of his entry into the other world.

For a while, he just sat on his bed, gripping it and waiting.

But still nothing happened.

There was no urge to do anything, no instinct to set the course in motion and he began to feel confused.

He'd never attempted to be in control before and he didn't know what to expect. On the first occasion, he'd been possessed by the force and it had driven his movements. He'd just been flotsam carried by the currents; and the second time he'd been asleep. Now it was as if he was waiting in some kind of limbo, with the controls to the time portal in his hand but without the knowledge of how to operate them.

And valuable seconds were going by.

Everything was in a state of stasis with time only being measured by the steady ticking of a clock that had no substance, and he was beginning to worry that Dad would come back. He'd find the spuds still sitting unpeeled on the draining board and his son in a trance on the bed. If that happened, he'd never live it down.

Eventually, he moved towards his bedroom door, still clutching the key and headed downstairs.

As he reached the hall, he heard another crash from the kitchen and the woman's voice shrieked again. This time he made sense of the words. "I don't know what's got into you, girl," he heard. "You carry on like this and you're heading for a whipping, do you understand?" It made him pull up short. It sounded as if all hell had broken loose beyond the kitchen door...but there was nothing there. He knew that – apart from a small pile of unpeeled spuds. All this was just sound from somewhere beyond reality, sound without substance, like the clock and the horses and the carts. Nothing about it was real.

At last he gripped the handle of the door and pushed through, still clinging to the key and still forcing the images from the past to the forefront of his mind.

But the moment he set foot inside the kitchen, the realisation hit him. All his intentions to be in control were going to be blown away.

A mind-numbing fury exploded around him and blanked every thought in his head. His brain turned to a buzz of cosmic blackness and his mind was held in the grip of such primeval violence that he was in control of nothing.

All he could do was grip the key, and with no power to do anything else, he staggered towards the door leading to the back yard.

Then he pushed the key against the door's surface.

He knew the forces outside would resist him, so he thrust with all his strength, and within seconds, he was sucked into the maelstrom. His cells disentangled and he was hurled pell-mell into a world that knew nothing of Jack O'Hagan or of his life or his times.

13

Jax had blanked out again. She was standing on the flagstones of the kitchen floor by the door leading to the yard. Yesterday's embers were still heaped in the hearth. They were cold and dead, and a November wind whipped under the door. As the confusion cleared, she groped for the dresser, feeling for a tinderbox and candles.

All night she'd been out pacing the cliffs through the woods and back. She'd sung her song and everything was as it had been last week, with shadows in the scrubland – tub carriers, batmen with their clubs, a procession of ponies, soaped and moving towards the cove, and all night, she'd been terrified at the thought of the fight when Barney and the dragoons attacked.

She'd seen the cutter and she'd seen galleys in the bay, but the dragoons never came and there'd been no fighting.

She had been aware of something unusual, although that wasn't in the cove or on the cliffs. It did have its effect though. There'd been confusion on the beach and everyone had fled, but the action that caused the confusion was far out in the bay. There'd been a second boat, very much like Mr Trelawny's cutter, but with a longer bowsprit, and when Mr Trelawny came to fetch her, he'd muttered something about a Revenue Cutter.

He didn't act as if he'd been routed by the other boat, and the dragoons hadn't arrested him as she'd hoped they would. He'd told her they'd sown the seed, and he said there'd be another time when the dust had settled – next week. They'd be out again then with a good set of creepers to finish the job.

Because the raid on the cliff hadn't happened and nothing had come about as Barney had said it would, she was confused. It also meant she was still trapped in the house and now she would have to plan another attempt at escape. She was determined to do this. She knew she couldn't walk those cliffs and perform those wicked enchantments again.

She couldn't understand what Mr Trelawny had told her on the cliff, but she clung to every word.

There was a part of her that was relieved nothing had happened. She'd been certain that if there was a fight out there, she would have been caught up in it and she would have been killed.

But now she was faced with new problems. Since Mr Trelawny was still here, her links to the dragoons left her even more vulnerable. She'd been to Polgarthen and she may have been seen.

There were two certainties in her head as she sparked the flint and set a candle in its stand. As long as she stayed in this house, she'd never be safe …and she wouldn't escape unless she got to Barney again.

She opened the door to the passage.

Mr Trelawny was standing at the end of the hall, cloaked and in shadows. He was by the long-cased clock.

Her main instinct, as she crept towards him, was for self-preservation and the first thing she needed to do was clear herself.

"Did I do wrong, master?" she whispered.

He lifted his head and stared. "Did you do what wrong, cheel?"

"The singin'. I charmed the boat my very best."

"You done all right, girl."

"Somethin' made you mad though," she said.

"It wasn't you, child. It was that other old boat, damn 'im."

He took off his cape and handed it to her. Then he said, "Give me a candle, girl. Then you can get off to bed, and don't you go frettin' about tonight. You done your part well enough. Next week, there'll be more for you to do. There'll be a dozen galleys workin' the cove then, and if you do your job well, there could be another sovereign in it for you."

But it was a long, slow week and every day there were visitors – the Squire and Mr Baldwyn and other men from the village.

None of them seemed worried about talking in front of her; but nothing they said made sense. Mostly, they talked about seeding and creeping up half ankers, and Cousin Jacky and liquor.

Then one day, when Mr Baldwyn was alone with Mr Trelawny, they took her down to the cellar.

The air was dank down there with a stench of rot. It scared her because there was a feeling about the place. It was so enclosed – four windowless walls and just the one unsubstantial stairway. Apart from the flickering areas where the candle flame reached, the darkness could be felt.

She watched as the two men groped around a pile of sacking, and as they pulled the sacks away, she saw a trapdoor. They opened it, and immediately there was a film of vapour – sea-spray hovering like dust clouds in the candlelight. There was a shaft plunging below the trap and metal rungs set into the rock. She guessed there must be a subterranean cavern down there. From its depths, she could hear the sea running in from the shore.

She stood, watching and listening.

She didn't understand creepers and half ankers, but she was certain they were linked to the contraband and now she was sure the two men were planning something involving the caverns. She had to get to her brother again. He had to be told…even though that might mean a raid on the house. She shuddered. The thought of fighting in the confines of that cellar was worse than the prospect of fighting on the cliff. It would put her in the deepest danger. There'd be no hiding place and it would leave her no route to escape.

But if she didn't get to Barney, if she didn't tell him about the caves, if Barney didn't do something to stop all this, she knew it could go on forever. She'd be a prisoner here, walking the cliffs as far into the future as she could see or until they found out she was the sister of a dragoon, and then it would be the end of her for certain.

For the next few days, her mind wrestled with the doubts and confusions.

She didn't know how she would get to Barney. And the fact that she'd already been in Polgarthen with a dragoon kept her constantly on edge.

There was something else too…and it wasn't something connected with the smuggling. But – if anything – this thing caused her more concern than all Mr Trelawny's activities.

It was connected with the fits.

The fit she'd had in the kitchen after they'd been out on the cliffs, had left her with that strange feeling of being possessed by another spirit again, only, this time, the feeling was stronger. She was constantly aware of the creature inside her and she knew it wasn't part of her. She could feel it now, and she had felt it ever since the morning of the fit. Sometimes, it seemed to be directing her thoughts. It was being her...and yet it wasn't being her.

She sensed the fits were opening the door to this thing. But the fits came in pairs and with the second fit, the thing would leave her and she would be her own self again. This time though, she hadn't had a second fit, and she could sense that the creature was beginning to feel trapped. As the week went on, it was getting more restless and there was a primitive, violent fear. It was as if it didn't want to be there, as if it was struggling to escape, and the thing's turbulent emotions mixing with her own thoughts kept her awake at night.

Like the creature inside her, she longed for another fit so it would go away.

Just over a week after the excise men had intercepted the cutter, they went out again, and with no moon, the night was almost black.

She was sent up onto the cliffs and she'd been instructed to sing. She had to grope in almost total blindness and all night, she sang:

"Ogh, gas dhymmo kres
My, y'n gedav gans es
Ke dhe gerdnes, ny vynnav vy mos.

A ny glewydh hy lev, a woles a sev
Y'n nansow ow kana mar deg."

As she stumbled over the protruding roots of trees and
the loose shale, she could sense the people around her
again – spots men, watching for the Revenue Men and
batmen, ready to fight if they turned up. This time she felt
there were even more and she was constantly aware of
the undergrowth alive with sinister shufflings. She could
hardly think straight, but she knew she must carry on
singing.

"Esedh dhymmo, sur, genev vy y'n leur
Yn-mysk an brialli y'n lann;
A ny glewydh hy lev, a woles a sev
Y'n nansow ow kana mar deg?"

She could barely make out any of the activity going on
at the foot of the cliff, but there were parts she could just
see because they'd lit fires down there at the entrance to
the caves below the woods. She could make out shapes
on the rocks and men staggering, carrying brushwood to
keep the fires alight. And in the light of the flames, she
could see a channel of seawater glinting, carved into the
rocks and running towards the cliff.

There were narrow galleys moving in and out of the
channel with their oars muffled, and the men worked all
night, carrying what looked like wooden barrels.

By the time Mr Trelawny came to fetch her, her body
ached with tiredness, but there was no relief.

He rushed her down the cliffside, pushing her roughly,
and he seemed impatient. "Come on, girl," he said. "Make
haste. We got to get you back, 'afore Mrs Spargo gets wind

you've been out. And when you get in, you can do up the fire. Then you can boil me some water so I can 'ave a bath. It's been a filthy night down there and I'm stiff with the cold."

She was hardly able to drag herself into the kitchen, she was so weary, and by the time she'd filled Mr Trelawny's bath, she could barely stand up.

She drew a sleeve across her eyes, and there was dew on her face, or mist or it may have been tears.

The night had been a morass of drudgery and misery as she had paced up and down the headland and she knew, whatever they'd planned last week – whatever Mr Trelawny had been talking about, the plans had now been carried out...and she hadn't been able to get to Barney. He still hadn't stopped the smuggling and it was too late now.

She was convinced as she went into the yard to draw water that she would be doomed to stay in this slavery to Mr Trelawny forever.

14

There wasn't any time to rest either. After Mr Trelawny had taken his bath and she'd emptied the water, she had to begin her chores, and that evening, she was called to the drawing room again.

Mr Baldwyn was there with Mr Trelawny. They were alone and Mr Baldwyn had an oily smile on his face. "Well done, my dear," he said. "That pretty song of yours came over clear as a bell last night. Now, fetch Mr Trelawny and me a drap of liquor, will 'ee?"

She didn't give much thought to what he'd said, but as she crossed to the dresser and picked up the decanter, her brain seemed to go out of control. There was no other explanation. She swung around, glaring at him. She was thinking, what right had Batty Batten to give her orders like that, especially in Mr Trelawny's house? He was well out of order. The guy was no more than a grovelling slug and there was no way she was going to be bossed around by the likes of him.

The shock of her sudden heretical thoughts nearly made her drop the decanter. She could hardly believe such words could have entered her mind. That insolent name, Batty Batten. She was uncomfortable with Mr Baldwyn, but she was in service to Mr Trelawny. Mr Baldwyn was

Mr Trelawny's guest, and it wasn't her place to question what he told her to do.

Fortunately, her gaping expression made Mr Trelawny laugh and he turned to Mr Baldwyn with a nod in her direction. "The cheel's a simpleton, Mr Baldwyn," he said. "She don't understand how to take orders from no one but me. Pour the brandy, girl, and then get back to the kitchen."

She found it hard to control her hands. What she'd just thought seemed to be almost in a foreign language. There were formations of words that weren't natural to her. It was the 'thing' in her head. It was taking control of her mind, making her think outrageous thoughts. And she was frightened that somehow, Mr Trelawny had known what she was thinking because he was staring at her, delving into his pockets. She flinched, but he was only taking out a sovereign and her muscles relaxed as he handed it to her. She was thankful that her impertinence hadn't been detected and she curtsied politely before heading for the door.

But then, without warning, she turned, thrusting her hands onto her hips in the most insolent way and with a voice that didn't have any part of her, she said: "Well, are you going to let me go to the bank with this like last time?"

Her effrontery amused Mr Baldwyn. "It's what they do say, Mr Trelawny," he said. "As thick as mules these maids, but put money their way and they're sharp as whippets."

"Well, are you?" she snapped. She couldn't stop herself. She knew her insolence was putting her life in danger, and at that moment, she just wanted to cut her own throat.

"If you've a mind to, girl," Mr Trelawny said, "safest place for it, Polglaise's Bank. But you leave the fixin' of it with me, and don't you go tellin' Mrs Spargo you've got no sovereign."

"That's all right then," she said. She scurried back to the kitchen, relieved that she was still in one piece, but she was dismayed by what was happening to her. When she got to the kitchen, she had to stand for a minute, clutching at the table.

What scared her most was that this madness seemed to come on her without warning. She was afraid it could happen at any time, and when it did happen, she had no control over it. She had no means of stopping it and that thought scared her very much.

Mrs Spargo was furious at having to take her to Polgarthen again. She treated her with cold fury, and on the day they went to market, she dumped her with hardly a word.

Jax still couldn't get used to the bustle and brutality of the market and she scanned the streets, desperate to see Barney. But there was no sign of him. Eventually, she drifted towards the alley where she'd met him last time. She could remember it because of the tavern and the ruffians lounging around outside.

Being in such proximity with the drunks again made her uneasy. She was afraid they might set on her like they had before, so after a few minutes, she made her way down between the houses. She was as unobtrusive as she could be for fear one of the louts would see her and take it as an invitation.

But as she came out onto the bank she heard a sharp hiss which frightened her. She swung around, only to see her brother lying on the grass, chewing a straw and holding a flagon of ale. It was such a relief that she let out a gasp of delight and he smiled at her. "I thought you might come back 'ere," he said. But when he caught sight of her face, he pulled up short and his expression clouded. "Are you all right? They treatin' you decent up there, are they?"

"Yes, why?" she said.

"Because you've got them great rims of darkness round your eyes. And you're lookin' real sick."

She laughed. She was so glad she'd found him. Now she could tell him everything. "That's me bein' tired. I was out doin' that ghost thing again a few nights ago."

When he heard that, he sat up. "They been out again?" he said. "And we missed it?"

"There wasn't anything like last time," she said. She settled beside him on the grass. "Only galleys rowin' in and out around the cliff. There wasn't no big boat. They was talking about seedin' the crop, and usin' creepers to bring in the Cousin Jacky."

He sighed. "So, that's what they've done."

She looked at him quizzically. "What's what they've done?"

"Creepin' up the tubs."

It was beginning to annoy her and she tore at a piece of grass. They all used the same language and it had no meaning. "I don't know what they've done," she snapped. "I don't know what any of it means – cousin Jacky, creepers, tubs. You're all talkin' riddles."

He leaned forward and jabbed the turf with his foot. "What I'm talkin' isn't riddles, sis. What I'm sayin' is this. They've outwitted us. When we boarded their cutter that night, she was clean. They must 'ave weighed the brandy barrels with stones and shot them overboard before we got there. That's what they mean by 'seedin' the crop'. Then, when the coast is clear, they go out with chains and grapplin' irons – creepers if you like – and fish the barrels up again. They'll 'ave stowed them away by now and we'll never lay our 'ands on them."

As he explained, what she'd seen from the cliffs suddenly made sense and she knew exactly where they'd taken the brandy. "No," she whispered. "You can find the barrels any time you want because I know where they've stowed them. I 'eard them plannin'. There's a cavern under Mr Trelawny's cellar with a channel runnin' in from the sea. That was where they were taking the barrels last week, using the rowing boats."

Barney looked at her intently. "Are you sure?"

"I seen the trapdoor down the cellar. There were rungs set in the rock going into the caverns. I could see the spray coming up. They made me go down with them to look at the cavern."

He grabbed her hand and his eyes were alive with excitement. "If that's true, sis, then we've got them. We can raid the place tonight before they shift the contraband out."

She watched him anxiously. He was silent now, perhaps thinking about something. At last he said, "You'll 'ave to give the housekeeper the slip this time, Martha, you can't go back. It won't be safe, you being in Trelawny's place, not with a raid going on in the house. I'll give you money so you can get back to mother."

It was what she'd wanted to hear more than anything in the world and the relief was so powerful she could have hugged him till there was no life left in him. Her eyes were welling up with gratitude, but then she opened her mouth and she heard her voice…it *was* her voice…even though the things it was saying weren't what she was thinking in any way.

She was all gratitude. She would be free of Tregenwyth and the terrifying walks across the cliffs. She was relieved because she wouldn't be dodging swords and bullets in the cellar – there'd be fighting and pistols down there, and there would be no place for her to hide. But what her voice said was: "No, Barney. I've got to go back. There's no way I can go to Penryn. And anyway, like you said, if I don't go back with the old woman, they'll be suspicious. They'll know something's up and they'll shift the loot before you get there."

She was rigid and she could feel the perspiration breaking out all over her face. She couldn't grasp how she could say anything so completely contrary to what she wanted.

She knew it was the thing inside her. She could sense it, and for some reason, it couldn't face the thought of moving away from Tregenwyth and Mr Trelawny's house. It seemed its life depended on it being there and it was just as it had been in the drawing room with Mr Baldwyn. It took over, ambushing her, saying words that were beyond her control, and the strange expressions it used – the way it spoke – none of it sounded like her. Nothing about it was her.

She could have wept. Barney's eyes grew wide.

"But there'll be soldiers, sis. Swarmin' all over the place, and there'll be shooting and fighting. I can't be certain we can keep you safe, not if you go back to Trelawny's."

It was a second chance and this time, she'd agree to his plans and go back to Penryn, but as she opened her mouth, all she heard was: "I've got to go back to Tregenwyth. Everything will go pear-shaped if I go down to Penryn. I've got to be in that house, don't you understand?"

It was as if she was going crazy and she felt the colour draining from her, especially when she saw Barney's expression.

She could see from how he looked that he was actually glad she was going back. What the voice had said made sense to him.

He didn't speak straightaway. He just stared at her and now, although she was desperate to unsay what she'd just said, her tongue wouldn't work. She stood there in abject misery; waiting for what she knew was coming.

At last he put his arm around her and he said, "Sis, you're the pluckiest maid as ever I knowed. You're a champion and I can tell you this, girl, I'm so proud of you, I can 'ardly speak. I promise you one thing. We'll do everything in our power to see you're safe. And you're right. If you had gone back to Penryn, the whole operation would have been scuppered. They'd have known something was up. You wouldn't have been safe. I know these people. They'd have hunted you down. They wouldn't have let you get away with betraying them and they would know for certain as soon as we raided the place."

She could have cried on the carrier's cart going back to Tregenwyth.

She had no idea what she was going to face that night, and if the prospect of the raid wasn't bad enough, Mr Trelawny was waiting for them when they arrived, demanding supper for him and the Squire and Mr Baldwyn.

All three of them would be there. And the fighting would be terrible.

Through the rest of the afternoon and into the evening, she felt she was walking on knife blades.

She helped Mrs Spargo prepare supper, and every time she heard a cart judder outside, or every time there was the heavy sound of a footfall on the cobbles, she nearly leapt out of her skin.

"What's got into you, girl?" Mrs Spargo snapped. "You're as jumpy as a mouse on heat."

She tried to hide it, but she couldn't get the thought of the impending raid out of her mind, and as the long-cased clock ticked the hours away, the tension tightened.

Part of her wanted to get the raid over before Mr Baldwyn and the Squire got there. If that happened, the fighting wouldn't be so bad. When any cart that paused outside the house started up again, whenever she heard the irascible neigh of a horse reluctant to do battle with the hill or when the heavy footsteps of a passer-by faded on the road, she felt disappointment.

When she did answer the door to a knock, it was the Squire. He came blustering in and he filled the hall with his massive frame so that even thinking about the loss of space drowned her in despair. Where would there be any place to hide in the approaching mayhem?

Then Mr Baldwyn arrived, and when she saw him, there was a menace hovering around him that set the thing inside her working in her brain again. Phrases like 'devious slug' and 'conniving rat' slid into her mind and that insolent name, Batty Batten…but still the raid didn't happen.

By now she was beginning to hope Barney and the customs men wouldn't come at all, that they'd leave it for another day or until the Squire and Mr Baldwyn had gone, when Mr Trelawny was in bed. If that happened, she would be safe in her attic room.

The three men were in cheerful spirits, laughing over their porter. She felt they were gloating at their successes; but then, just after she'd filled their glasses with a good wine and was carrying in a terrine of soup...it happened – a thunderous banging on the door that made Mr Trelawny leap out of his chair, and she was so scared, she nearly dropped the terrine.

"Who'd be coming here makin' that kind of a racket this time of night?" he demanded. He turned to her, his features twisted with irritation. "Go and see who it is, cheel. And send them about their business. I don't want no interruptions during supper. Villains bangin' on my door, this time of night! I'll 'ave them up at the next assize."

But sending them about their business wasn't an option. She had hardly lifted the latch when the first of the customs men were through. They were followed by a whole stream, shouldering past her and pushing her against the wall.

She struggled to see if she could recognise Barney, but there were so many of them, and it all happened so quickly. The chaos and confusion were even worse than she'd imagined.

Mr Trelawny came storming into the passage, his face twisted with fury and snarled, "What in the devil's name is goin' on 'ere?"

One of the soldiers stared at him. "Mr Trelawny?" he said.

"The same, sir. In 'is own house, tryin' to entertain decent, respectable folk."

Jax could barely breathe, and the soldier didn't take any notice of what Mr Trelawny had said. He just stood there squarely and carried on speaking. "I believe, sir, you're harbouring contraband and we're 'ere in the King's name to search until it be found."

Even though the flickering lamplight was dim, she could see Mr Trelawny's face darken. He banged his fist against the wall and shouted, "How dare you, sir! I'll have you know you're in one of the most respectable houses in the county. Would it interest you to know, sir, that I'm enetertainin' a magistrate at this very moment and the proprietor of the largest countin' house in Cornwall. Not the kind of persons to 'ave truck with contraband!"

What he said made her tremble. She began to wonder if she'd got it wrong. What would he and a magistrate and the proprietor of a bank want with free traders?

But the soldier wasn't impressed. He just repeated his accusations and then he said, "My men are here, sir, to search your house until the contraband be found."

After that, the dragoons swarmed everywhere, bounding up the stairs, into the attic, into the bedrooms, into the library, into the drawing room. They burst into the kitchen, and Mrs Spargo came out screaming, wringing her hands and yelling: "Lord 'ave mercy, Mr Trelawny, sir. There's soldiers running amuck in my kitchen."

Mr Trelawny turned to the chief Revenue Man and snarled: "There is no contraband in this house, sir. And I promise you, every man-jack of you will be up before Mr Baldwyn here at the next assize if you do not remove this rabble from my property this instant."

But the Revenue Man didn't flinch. All he said was, "Do you have a cellar, Mr Trelawny?"

That made Jax cling to the wall in blind terror. They'd all be down there in that confined space, in darkness, with swords flashing and pistols shooting.

All she wanted to do was stay where she was, anchored to the passage floor, while the carnage went on below her. But she couldn't. She was caught up in the surge of bodies and she was driven, with no way of escape as the soldiers stormed down the steps.

It was a mass of confusion in the cellar, with men shouting and bodies pushing at each other.

A few of the soldiers struck flints and lit tapers, and in the flickering light, Jax could make out Mr Trelawny and the Squire at the foot of the stairs being jostled. They were both shouting strings of abuse at the dragoons.

The trapdoor was hidden under sacking and as her eyes struggled to take in the mayhem, she saw Mr Baldwyn push through until he'd placed himself precisely over it. He seemed to be trying to block its entrance, preventing the soldiers from discovering it, but immediately one of the dragoons sprang into action. And Jax swallowed her breath, because she recognised the dragoon's voice.

It was Barney.

"Move, sir," he snapped.

"Move? Why should I move?" Mr Baldwyn growled.

She saw her brother as calm as ice standing in front of him. "Because, sir, we've been told to search everywhere," he said. Then he gave him a shove, kicking the sacks away...and there was a shout of triumph as he lifted the trapdoor.

The shout was followed by a metallic glint and one blinding flash from Mr Baldwyn's pistol. It echoed around the cellar with ear-splitting precision, and after that, in Jax' head, there was nothing but silence.

It was as if the whole world had frozen and she didn't think she could draw breath.

Then all around her, the air began rushing, and her body was being torn apart as if the forces of retreating time were drawing her out of herself and in the maelstrom of confusion, she fell…

And as she hit the ground, a most deathly calm crept over her.

15

Jack was lying on the kitchen floor by the door. He was sprawled out and he knew it had happened again. But this time something was different. Although the memories were already dissolving into sludge, something was staying with him.

Things had taken place back there, in the cellar – things that had scared him, the ear-splitting crack of a pistol and a blinding flash of light and whatever had happened, it seemed to touch the skin of death.

There'd been confusion in the cellar too – a chaotic miasma of moving figures, shadowy, ill-defined and after that, an out-of-earth experience of silence.

There were still no names and no clearly defined faces except for that of Batten.

He knew Batten had been back there and he suspected it was him who had fired the pistol. The events leading up to these happenings though, were still no clearer than when he'd come back at other times.

But there was something about being trapped this time and that had been a big thing for him.

He was sure now that access to the portal involved locked doors and his use of the key. It was the key that got him back there. But he was also beginning to realise the key only took him into the past. It had no power to re-open the portal to the present.

While he'd been back this time, he was aware that some part of him had been very frightened. There'd been a feeling of helplessness and imprisonment. It was still setting the adrenaline racing in his veins.

It hadn't been a brief visit this time either. He'd been gone for nearly a fortnight and he'd been desperate to escape.

He sat up, leaning against the door, and glanced around the kitchen. What if he hadn't managed to come back? What if whatever controlled his return, had taken it into its head not to release him? What would have happened to him back here in his own time if that had happened?

Would he have remained slumped against the door as he had been a minute ago? Would he have stayed in some coma until his body withered and died?

He looked more closely around the room.

He must have been lying here for nearly two weeks.

His dad must know what had happened. He would have come back from his shopping and found him slumped against the door and he would have called Mum.

He imagined her scorching up the miles between Polgarthen and here. She would have had him back in hospital…

But he wasn't in hospital.

He was still on the kitchen floor. And all around him he was conscious of a silence. It seemed to have gripped the whole universe and he couldn't understand it.

He shouldn't be here. There was no way his mum and dad would just leave him, carrying on around him as if his inert body, prostrate by the back door, was of no consequence.

Perhaps, every time he went back, his body disappeared so all his dad would have found when he returned from shopping was an empty house.

That would be it. They were out now looking for him, probably getting the police involved.

He staggered to his feet and stared at the key.

This key was the gateway…but the gateway to what? And if it was of no use in bringing him back to the present…

He shuddered. He was beginning to realise just how dangerous all this was.

Next time he turned the key in a locked door, he could be opening a portal into his own destruction.

He didn't know what to do.

Without the key, he couldn't go back and there were things going on back there that he was convinced were important. Besides, the business of Batten being in both times was affecting the stability of the house. It was interfering with the smooth running of his life. If he didn't go back again, if he didn't get to the root of all this…

Part of him was certain he'd never have any peace if he didn't get to grips with it, and yet…every time he took this trip, it was putting his life on the line. That was too dangerous. It was dicing with death.

His brain was oscillating between two propositions; but his instinct was beginning to tell him that 'now' was the only safe place to be. The memory beyond those locked doors had the smell of death about it – flashes of cracking pistols, the stench of spent gunpowder – and the terror of being imprisoned back there, unable to return to his own time. It was something he hadn't been aware of before, and it horrified him. The only way to guarantee he'd never put himself at such risk again was to ditch the key. If he did that, he wouldn't have access to the portals next time the house became unstable.

It was a big decision. Getting rid of the key would mean he'd never be free of these premonitions and the déjà vu; the noises and images from the other world would be with him for as long as he lived.

He felt the roughness of the key's corrosion in his hand and slowly, his footsteps were leading him to the back door.

Every instinct of self-preservation screamed in his head. Better to endure the hauntings of déjà vu than risk rotting in some coma, lost in the other world, and as he was thinking, he pushed the door open. Then, with one sweep of his hand, he hurled the key into the air.

His eyes were closed, but he could hear the metal ricochet against the wall at the back of the yard as the key fell fractiously between branches of honeysuckle and clematis. With a dull thud, it found the ground, and he knew it was lost forever in the tangle of undergrowth.

For a moment, he stood there, his heart thumping, but inside, the euphoria of freedom was bubbling up, as if a death sentence had been lifted. No matter how much the house haunted him, from now on, it couldn't drag him back to that dangerous past.

He closed the door to the yard and looked around him, rubbing his hands.

His next move should be to inform the police that he was no longer 'missing'; but just as he was about to leave the kitchen, he glimpsed the pile of unpeeled potatoes and the potato peeler just as he'd left them a fortnight ago ...and that didn't make sense. Those spuds shouldn't still be there.

Even if his mum and dad were eaten up with grief over his disappearance, they wouldn't have left a pile of unpeeled potatoes on the draining board for nearly two weeks.

For one thing, if they'd been there for that long, they'd have started going mangy, but they were just as they'd been before he went back, fresh, with their skins still shining, and it seemed as if nothing had been touched.

It was an eerie thought and suddenly, the silence around the house began to take on a different feeling. It was the feeling of time in stasis again.

He couldn't even hear the tick of the long-cased clock, and as he looked around, he felt anxious.

Something else had happened while he'd been on this trip.

He went across to the sink and picked up one of the potatoes. It was firm and unyielding. Then he glanced at the hook on the door. The re-usable shopping bag that Dad had taken with him was still missing. It was almost as if his father hadn't come back.

While Jack had been away, time must have been suspended and he had this uneasy feeling that for everyone else, it still was suspended. He was the only one in the whole world alive and moving.

He could feel cold fear on his face and a film of perspiration that was near panic.

He couldn't move for a moment and then he went into the passage.

He pushed open the front door and glanced into the street. Shadows still invaded the hill with gangling houses shutting off the rays of sunlight, but there was the same eerie stillness even here. There wasn't even a twitch of a curtain across the road from Gladys Miners' window.

He turned back and went into the lounge. He felt sick.

He needed conclusive proof and an idea occurred to him.

The television would give him his answer.

If time really was suspended, he'd have a frozen picture or a screen that was completely blank.

He pressed the remote, powering up the digital box and waited anxiously, but as the set found a channel, the screen burst to life.

The television had been tuned to BBC News and there was an immediate chatter of a reporter outside Parliament. She was interviewing some protestors objecting to the latest declaration of cuts, and at the bottom of the screen, the ribbon was running, displaying the time.

He gasped.

Whatever day it was, the digital clock displayed a time only a few minutes after his dad had left the house. He took out his iPhone. The date displayed was the very same as the day when he'd come out of hospital.

Time was not standing still. The two weeks of torment in the other world had barely displaced a single second of real time. His mum was at work in Polgarthen. His dad was still on his way to the shops and everything was as normal as it could be. He'd got time to peel the spuds before his dad got back. He might even do something fancy with them for lunch just to show his cynical father that he was his equal when it came to culinary matters.

He'd seen his dad in operation and what he did wasn't witchcraft. *Pomme de Terre au Gratin;* he thought. He could do that. He'd chop the potatoes into slices, parboil them and layer them between grated cheese, and he'd have the whole thing in the oven by the time his dad got back.

That would teach him to mock Jack's culinary potential.

The fact that time hadn't frozen and that he was now back in his own life rhythms, together with the knowledge that he'd ditched the key, lifted his spirits and he almost felt light-headed as he set about peeling the potatoes. He was ready to take on any challenge.

He found a saucepan and a dish to lay out his creation. Then he fetched a packet of grated cheddar from the fridge. He knew it was there because he remembered buying it in Spar earlier in the week.

He left the sliced potatoes boiling for five minutes, and while he was waiting, he cleared away the peelings and wiped down the surfaces.

He was slightly unnerved that these tasks came so naturally. He must have had more of his dad's genetic structure than he'd been prepared to acknowledge. He wanted it to be that. The alternative was too unpalatable to think about. If it wasn't his dad's inherited genes, it had something to do with these trips into the past. Every time he went back, he sensed that his life back there was bound up in domestic chores. If it was the past that was influencing his life, that freaked him out. He'd prefer it to be his dad's genes.

Whatever the cause, messing about in the kitchen wasn't a big deal and the sting seemed to have been drawn from his view of Dad's pre-occupations.

Besides, what did it all matter? He could do what he liked in the kitchen – as long as he still knew he was a guy through and through – and some of the best chefs were men.

He drained the potatoes and layered them in the dish. He'd put a bed of grated cheese in first. Then he put down more cheese and another layer of potatoes. After that, he stood back and admired his handiwork.

That would impress his dad.

But impressing Dad wasn't really enough. What he really wanted to do was blow his mind. He'd spice up this *Pomme de Terre* thing so that it would really send his dad's head spinning. He'd add a shot of wine – white wine – that's what his instinct told him would perk up potatoes and cheese.

The wine was in the cellar. He'd get a bottle now, slurp it over his creation and get it in the oven before Dad got back.

As he reached the bottom cellar step, though, memories started flooding back, and he wasn't prepared for the immediacy. It was as if he'd been there just minutes ago, and the images that were flashing around his head weren't of his time. In his mind, he could see soldiers – redcoats, pushing and surging like sea currents, and there was a tension in the air of apprehension and panic. He heard the gunfire again and saw the flash of an exploding pistol. For a second, the shock made him stagger and his confidence and relief at being back in the twenty-first century was shaken. It was as if the house had seized him and he grasped at the lime-covered wall for support.

But after the first disorientating moment, he pulled himself back. He had to get a grip on himself. He was down in the cellar in an age where he and his mate Terry lazed the days away, fishing and lounging on hidden beaches where holidaymakers milled about the waterfronts and souvenirs and good feelings were the prime forces.

This was not a place of horror and death. He was down here for a bottle of white wine, and that was the fact he must cling to.

He went to the wine rack and pulled out bottles until he found one that appeared to have white wine in it.

"Dry and fruity", the label said. That should work. He'd put a splash in the dish and keep the rest in the fridge so Dad could have it with his lunch.

As he stood there reading the label, the oppressive feeling about the past paled, even though he still didn't feel at ease. But then, he froze. He could hear the incessant surge of the sea probing the caverns, but there was more – the voices were there again, deep below the cellar floor.

He listened, trying to catch the words. It was a cacophony – raised, angry voices merging together. They seemed to be arguing, but the noise was muffled by the thickness of rock and he couldn't make out a recognisable pitch.

He wondered if the voices were foreign. Then he heard one voice raised above the rest, and that made his spine rigid because that voice, he recognised. Batty Batten was down there, dictating the odds. He could hear him swearing and cursing, and at the same time, there was a surging rush of the déjà vu.

To the right of where he stood by the wall in the corner, he knew there would be a trapdoor – one that would lead down into the caverns. He'd seen it opened by Batten and another guy, a big heavy man in breeches and a smoking jacket, a man with wisps of grey hair, lank and escaping from under a pill box cap. And again, he'd seen it opened when the soldiers were swarming and there'd been a young soldier involved this time. He had been by the trap with Batten, and Jack felt this young guy was somehow special. It was while all this was happening that the gun had been fired…and the trapdoor…he knew exactly where it was.

He put the bottle down by the rack and went across.

Then with his foot, he cleared the dust away, along with the accumulation of centuries of rubble, and…it was there, a square of beaten iron with a corroded metal ring – a door that would lead down to the subterranean maze of caverns. He felt unnerved. To know things like this wasn't natural, but he bent down all the same…and then…he stopped. If he opened the door while the cellar light was on, it would shine through and Batty Batten with his marauding crowd would see it.

He'd have to get a torch. He took the bottle of wine and clambered back to the passage.

The eerie silence still hung over the house and in the hot breathlessness of summer heat, although now, shrouded in the stillness, he could hear the faint ticking of the long-cased clock again, and with the clock, came the reminder that the past was still there, hovering just beyond his consciousness. It had not gone away even though he'd ditched the key.

He went into the kitchen and put the bottle of wine beside his prepared dish of potatoes. Then he crossed to the cupboard for a torch.

Once he'd returned to the cellar, he switched off the light and found the trap again, using only the torch's beam.

He switched the torch off and the chilly blackness made his pupils stretch. In the darkness, he groped for the metal ring, hooking his finger into it, and with his eyes still straining, he pulled gently.

The trap was stiff, but eventually, it gave, and he eased it on its hinges.

As soon as it was open, he could feel the spray from the sea breathing on his face and there was the coldness of salt stinging his eyes.

He peered down. It was a deep recess of confusion, but with the trapdoor open, the voices suddenly became clearer and so did the undulation of the sea-swell.

He stared and gradually, as his eyes adjusted, he could make out dark, shadowy figures. There were men with torches down there, and he could see something that looked like more permanent lighting set in the walls across the other side of the cavern.

The light glinted on the tips of the waves, and he could see the figures clustered together on the dimly illuminated ledges. There were small boats rocking in channels. He could only make them out as ill-defined shapes, but they were visible, shunting around in the water. He couldn't identify the language of the voices, apart from the words yelled out by Batty Batten who was watching the rabble from a more distant vantage point, cursing and swearing in unmistakable English. Then he shouted something in the same unfamiliar language that the rest were using and it was clear from watching them that whatever operation was going on, Batten was in control, and his voice, especially in the foreign dialect, was harsh and evil.

Jack closed the trapdoor again. He'd seen enough.

There was nothing he could do with that lot running riot in the cavern, but his curiosity was aroused.

He'd have to come back. He'd come with Terry this afternoon perhaps or at some time when both his parents were out.

There would be a time when the coast was clear down there. The voices weren't always there. When the caves were empty, they would go down and find out exactly what Batten and Greg were doing, find out who these people were with their unrecognisable dialect and their repressed violence, get to the truth of what evil Batten was involved in here in the twenty-first century.

16

The adrenaline was still setting him on fire as he went back to the kitchen, but because there was nothing he could do in the caverns, he had to channel the surplus energy into cooking. He splashed wine over his cheese and potato creation, then put the dish in the oven. He decided he'd set the oven to 'moderate'. That would make sure it wouldn't cook too fast and the potatoes would brown, but wouldn't burn.

He checked that everything was cleared away. He'd already wiped down the work surfaces but he thought another quick going over wouldn't come amiss, and the cheese bag needed binning. The wine had to be re-corked too and put in the fridge so it would be chilled for Dad's lunch.

It didn't bother him that he was following this domestic path, and if he was honest, what he'd just done gave him satisfaction. It wasn't something he'd be sharing with Terry, and he'd make sure his dad didn't go broadcasting it in inappropriate circles, but it was a good feeling.

When the kitchen was clear, he went up to his bedroom and lay on the bed. Last night he hadn't slept properly. Hospital wasn't the kind of place you could sleep easily, and now that the excess of adrenaline had been spent, the trauma of going back in time and the experience of finding Batten in the caves was beginning to leave its mark. He felt exhausted.

Most of the raging instabilities in the house seemed to have been neutralised by his visit to the past.

He'd noticed that before. It was almost like a pattern: first, a build-up of tension, then the compulsion to use the key in some immoveable door. It seemed to be constructed into cycles designed to thrust him back through the time portal. But each time, after he'd been back, the instability lost its fury and the house returned to some sort of normality until the next cycle began.

The tension never completely went away.

Even as he lay there, the morning's stillness had a presence about it. It hovered over the house, shrouding it with hints of dormant menace. It wasn't an easy atmosphere, and from downstairs, he was aware of the ticking clock marking off the passing of time.

The clock was a constant presence, an emissary from the past, demarking a gradual build-up to next explosion and he didn't know what would happen next time, not now that he'd got rid of the key. That made him uneasy. But he was determined. Going back wasn't an option, not when his return to the present was so far out of his control.

He was feeling restless about Batten too. The thought of those people down in the cavern disturbed him deeply. It was as if they'd invaded his personal space, and they sounded like a rough bunch. He felt this rent-a-mob had the potential to be lethal.

He closed his eyes, mulling over what he'd seen, but he was listening for the door as well, and when he heard the click of a key in the Yale lock, he pulled himself up from the bed. He wanted to witness his dad's reaction to his creativity in the kitchen. And he wasn't disappointed. As soon as Dad shoved through the door, he sniffed.

"Did I put something in the oven before I left?" he said. "Because there's a pretty good smell around here."

"Would it be my new deodorant?" Jack said as he came grinning, down the stairs. "I mean, there's nothing like a good squirt to cover up the old body pong."

Dad chuckled. "Nothing, apart from a shower now and again, but it takes a lot to get boys of your age to understand that, doesn't it, Jacky boy? I mean, a stink under the armpit, a quick squirt with a spray can – much better than the indignities of shower gel and water."

"Makes sense to me," Jack said, shrugging, but Dad was still sniffing.

"I've never smelled a deodorant perfumed with the delicacies of good cooking though. I must have put something on, but I don't remember."

"Go in the kitchen and see." There was a bit of Jack that was really enjoying this. "I've peeled the spuds like you said, keeping the inside bits and ditching the skins. That okay?"

His dad sighed. "And I'll bet the place is looking like a bomb's hit it," he said.

He pushed the kitchen door open and Jack stood behind him, chuckling with pleasure. His father had stopped in mid-stride and he turned, staring. "Good Lord! This place is cleaner than I left it," he said. But then, he scanned the room and a mocking half-smile glimmered on his face. "The potatoes, though – it looks as if you've ditched the insides as well as the outsides."

Jack pushed past him, grabbing a glove and opening the oven door. He pulled out his dish of cheese and potato. "*Pomme de Terre au Gratin*," he said. "I'm not just a pretty face." And his dad's expression made everything worthwhile.

His mouth was open like a stuck goldfish and that look matched his eyes.

He staggered to a kitchen chair in an act of exaggerated shock. "This is not the son I fathered," he gasped. "And wine! I can smell the hints of wine in the cooking."

Jack was still smiling. "Just a dash of white to liven up the taste. I've put the rest in the fridge to chill for lunch."

His father had no words and that made Jack bristle with triumph. He'd managed to silence the most prolific son of the Blarney Stone this side of County Cork.

"So, no more comments about me needing a manual to boil a kettle, okay?"

"My lips are sealed," Dad said and Jack headed for the door.

The right exit was always a matter of timing and this, he thought, was the perfect time. "That'll be a first then," he said. "I'm going down to the harbour for half an hour to catch up with Terry."

"Well, be back for lunch," said Dad. "What time will your creation be ready?"

"Just keep an eye on it." Jack moved towards the front door. All this talk of the culinary arts was getting a bit weird. "When the potatoes turn to a golden brown and start to crisp, then it's ready. Don't worry. I'll be back."

"Well, see that you are," his father called. "I need to be in Polgarthen this afternoon, and I don't want to be hanging around waiting for you to show."

Jack turned for the harbour, relieved to be outside, glad of his first moments of freedom since his internment in hospital.

He was pleased Dad was going into Polgarthen. It meant that, provided the coast was clear down in the cavern, he and Terry could do a bit of investigating.

He ambled through to the open quayside and as he left the claustrophobic grip of the hill, the full strength of the early August sun burst on him with the bay's vista of sparkling seas stretching to the horizon, and the buzz of tourist activity lifted him to a higher sphere of motivation.

Finding Terry wasn't difficult. The guy was more predictable than sunrise.

He was on his punt, bare-backed and bronzed, working on his lines.

Jack called across to him and he looked up, beckoning him onto the boat.

They arranged for Terry to come up at half past two after Jack's dad had left for Polgarthen.

"You really seen Batten down there?" he said as he shouldered through the front door. "You certain it was 'im with those foreign guys?"

It was as if the questions had been buzzing in his head since Jack had told him that morning.

"Yeah, I'm certain. I'd recognise his voice anywhere. There was this tension down there. They were shouting at each other, and some of the time it sounded as if Batten was talking their language. I couldn't understand what they were saying, but the way they said it, short, snappy, usually just one or two syllables, it was like they were cursing and swearing most of the time."

Terry paused and peered around. "Rambling old place, this, isn't it?" he said. "Never been in 'ere before."

"It's seriously old," said Jack. "Dad reckons it's well over four hundred years. He says it's got character and history, but…" He tailed off. He had hoped Terry would sense the same things about the place that he was sensing, but it didn't happen. Terry had the normal reaction to a rambling old building.

"How many floors?" he asked, peering up the gyration of the staircase, and Jack laughed.

"You tell me. The way the place is designed, there's hardly one room on the same level as another. I guess three, and then there's the attic."

"And this cellar," Terry said. "How did you know to get down to the caverns?"

"Just sort of found out," Jack said with a shrug.

"We going down there then? Best see if the coast is clear first. I mean, it wouldn't be no good goin' right down into the caves and then stumbling over a load of foreign speakin' desperadoes. Do you reckon it's them that duffed up the Greg guy?"

"It wasn't Batten and that's for sure," Jack said. "I'll get a torch."

He could still see glimpses of the rampaging soldiers in the cellar, but to Terry, it was just another cellar and that, somehow, disappointed Jack.

They paused on the stairs and Terry held up his hand. Then he laughed. "You're right," he said. "You can 'ear the sea down 'ere. That's weird." He was peering around. "Where's this trapdoor then?"

Jack led him to the back wall. He shone the torch onto the small square of hinged metal and listened for a minute.

Then he handed Terry the torch. "Turn off the light," he said. He was speaking quietly now, for fear the rabble might still be down there. "Then come back here and I'll lift the trap. But you'll have to switch the torch off. If those guys are still down there, they'll see any light from up here. We've got to be dead quiet too."

Terry nodded and chuckled. "'Aven't done nothin' this excitin' in years. You're like a breath of fresh air round the place, simple Jack. The biggest thrill I've 'ad up till now is scrumpin' apples and skinny dippin' out Three Corners' Cove."

He went across and switched off the light. Then, with his way illuminated by the torch, he came back to where Jack was crouched over the trap door.

Jack groped, lifting the squared off piece of rough iron, swinging it open on its hinges, and immediately, the cold salt of the spray touched his face, and the noise of the sea washing the channels below changed from a muted blur to clear undulating surges. The sound echoed around the chasms, rising and falling and Terry gasped.

"That's awesome," he whispered.

They peered into the void, watching for movements or a glimmer of light, and as their eyes adjusted, they could make out a slight greying where light from the cave's entrance filtered in. Shrouded in mists, there were suggestions of motion as the water rose and fell in the channels below. But there was no sign of human activity; none of the wandering torch beams, and the lights in the cave wall that Jack had seen earlier weren't on anymore.

"I don't think there's anyone down there," he whispered. He waited for a few more minutes to reassure himself. Then he took the torch and shone it into the blackness of the shaft.

The beam pierced the void, its rays broadening into a path of yellow, penetrating the haze of water vapour. It just managed to find the bottom of the cavern and it etched out ribbons of wavelets advancing and retreating in the maze of channels.

Then he moved the beam of light so that it shone towards the walls, but it must have been vast down there, because the light just dissolved into spray and infinite blackness, and all the time, the sea sucked and swelled.

"I think it's okay," he whispered. "Let's go."

"How?" said Terry. "We abseiling or what?"

Jack focused the torch onto the back of the trap. There was a wall of rock descending, damp and gleaming, and he could see rusting staples of iron set into the rock. They were steps to the abyss. He'd known they would be there.

He put his foot on the first rung.

"Careful," Terry whispered. "Some of them things look rusted through. Test them out before you put your full weight on them."

He began his descent, feeling tentatively, gripping the iron struts above him as a precaution. Terry followed and Jack's heart was pounding. Even with Terry there, this was almost an adventure too far. It was so dark, and the chill of the caves clawed at his face.

He realised that if the guys were still down there or if one of them came back, there would be no chance of making a retreat. It would be impossible to find the ladder again if there was a chase. It was in his head to suggest they give up and go back to the comparative security of the cellar. There was still the memory of a gun flash over the trap entrance and a realisation that at some point, a body must have plummeted down this shaft. For all he knew, its remains could still be lying there, cold and rotten on the rocks below.

It was a long climb too, and even in this dank coldness, his hands were clammy, but at last his foot felt the surface of a rock and he stepped away, allowing space for Terry.

They scanned the cavern with the torch and it was clear the place had been doctored at some time to make it user friendly. There were flattened levels of rocks with stumps of posts that had been used for moorings. Boats must have been brought up here and what surprised Jack was, the mooring places were clearly under their house, and they were very old.

He stood on one of the makeshift jetties and shone the torch down the channel. "What's all this, do you reckon?" he asked.

Terry was standing beside him staring around and here in the depths, the strength of the sea swell made surging crescendos, struggling to rolling climaxes with the constant rhythm of the waves, and the noise echoed to the distant walls. "Smugglin'," he said. "The place was rife with it a couple of centuries back. They must 'ave run some sort of operation from up in your 'ouse."

Jack blinked as yet another piece of the past fell into place. Soldiers and men shooting their pistols, people, including Batten's other persona, dressed for the eighteenth century – this dark past that was haunting him must have had something to do with smuggling…and now Batten was at it again.

He shone the torch across to the other channels, the ones running under the choirmaster's house, and both boys drew breath simultaneously. Where the channels forged their way below Batten's cellar, there were jetties – not rough-hewn flattenings of rocks, but concrete jetties with iron railings and moorings, with steps down to the channels and a set of rougher steps climbing to a clearly defined shaft. The shaft ran from the main wall of the cavern and it looked as if it was heading west, probing beneath the village in the direction of Trelawny's Wood. It was raised well above sea level. And further along, there was scaffolding, carrying steps directly into Batten's cellar.

"Take a look at that," Terry whispered. "There's something going on down 'ere, Jack, mate – bigger than you and me ever imagined. Where do that shaft go?"

Jack's heart was pounding, not so much with fear, but with the thrill of discovery. It was a vindication of all he'd ever felt about Batten. "Let's take a look," he said.

They followed the beam of the torch, treading carefully.

"I told you that guy was no good," Terry said. "Think this is some sort of smugglin' operation do 'ee?"

"It's got to be," said Jack. He nearly added: "*Batten's a past master of smuggling. He's been involved in it for centuries.*" But he stifled the remark. Its truth though, was burning inside him.

The shaft, when they got to it, was dry, and the floor was worn with footmarks; some of them recently imprinted into the compressed earth. They were men's footprints and occasionally there was other evidence of human habitation – discarded litter, empty boxes, cigarette packets, drinks cartons and the like. Jack bent down to pick up one of the discarded cigarette packets and examined it. The writing on it wasn't English, and on some of the packets, the lettering seemed to be in a kind of Arabic script. "What do you make of that?" he said, showing the packet to Terry.

Terry shook his head. "Africans. Don't mean nothin' to me."

Carefully, they edged forwards, watching all the time for signs of life ahead of them.

The floor was level and the shaft seemed to have a certain uniformity as if it had been carved out of the rock and shale by hand.

"We goin' to see where this leads?" Terry said, but Jack didn't answer. He was almost afraid to verbalise what they were doing, and he edged deeper into the tunnel.

There was no way of assessing how far they'd got, and everywhere, there was evidence of occupation, but then Jack stopped and grabbed Terry by the arm. His heart was thumping and an ice-cold sensation crept across him. In the far distance, around a bend in the path, beyond the reach of the torch's beam, he heard voices, much the same as those he'd heard this morning. He turned to Terry, swinging back to where they'd come from.

"Quick," he whispered. "There's still people down here. Let's get out."

Terry didn't need any persuading and they legged it down the shaft to the cavern, groping across the rocks until they reached the foot of the ladder.

"There are things I've got to tell you about those guys," Jack panted as he began to climb. "They are seriously dangerous. Greg's in hospital, pretty near on life-support. He came in before I left this morning and I think those guys are responsible. If they caught us down here, I wouldn't give much for our chances."

He heard Terry swear under his breath. Then he began to follow Jack. "I got you," he whispered. "Let's get out of 'ere while we're still in one piece."

17

When they reached the relative safety of the cellar, there wasn't a lot more they could do.

Jack filled Terry in about Greg's injuries, and Terry whistled through his teeth.

"It isn't safe goin' down in them caves," he said. "If we're goin' to find out about all this, we've got to do it from the cliffs. I mean, if they done that to Greg, and they meet up with us in that tunnel, we aren't going to stand a chance."

"I may be able to get a clearer idea of what's going on if I watched them sometimes from the trapdoor," Jack said. "If I opened the door without the cellar light on, they wouldn't know I was there. They've got all those lights down there, so I could see what was happening and sometimes, I suppose, Batten will say something intelligible in English, although this morning he was talking the same language as them."

"What do you think 'ee's up to?" Terry said.

Jack shrugged. "Smuggling. It's got to be — drugs or something — but what I don't understand is, why he needs all those guys if he's just smuggling drugs. And that crowd — they're like — seriously violent. He can hardly control them."

They set out for the harbour, leaving a note for Jack's father explaining that they'd gone fishing and that Jack would be back with mackerel for supper.

"Do 'ee think the cave could be linked with the mine shafts out by Trelawny's Wood?" Terry asked. "They could be workin' one of them mines up behind Three Corners' Cove – doin' it illegally."

"I thought the tin mines were spent," said Jack.

"They stopped usin' them. But that was because the price of tin dropped. There's still tin in there and copper and arsenic. And there's gold too, they do reckon."

"The only way we're going to find out is if we follow Batten over the cliffs," Jack said.

They strolled down towards the quayside and Jack's head was spinning.

He was glad of the normality and warmth of the bay and the chance to relax, and an afternoon in the bay worked its usual magic. Terry powered the punt out through the harbour gap and they fished on into the early evening.

It was too late by the time they got back to Tregenwyth, to follow Batten and reddened by the salt and the sun, and tired from fishing, Jack was hoping, for once, that the mood in the house would just ease off a bit. He longed for the unbroken sleep of healthy exhaustion. And, although the breathless silence of the hill still held portents of instability, and the house maintained its shroud of a secret past, the mood did seem more docile.

He went to bed early because he was genuinely tired.

He felt more able to rationalise things now and he hoped that meant the tension wouldn't impinge on his sleep so much.

He knew there'd been smuggling operations going on around the house two or three centuries ago, with Batten and possibly some guy called Trelawny involved. It explained the fighting in the cellar and the gunfire. Although he was still disturbed by the knowledge that somehow, all this was tied into his own life, he felt more secure. He was certain he'd got rid of the only means of going back, and that meant he wasn't in the same kind of danger from the instabilities. He was also genuinely tired; too tired to allow these things to unsettle him. For the time being, the trauma had lost its edge. Even the non-existent clock in the hall, ticking away the hours, didn't bother him, and he slept through, on the edge of peace until morning.

For the next few days, investigating Batten seemed less urgent.

The summer heat was unrelenting and he found that his newly symbiotic relationship with dad, helping with the housework and performing the odd culinary masterpiece in the kitchen, earned him freedom to go off for long afternoons with Terry, taking the punt and exploring the coves on either side of Tregenwyth.

His preference was to go east of the village.

Passing the cliff up by Trelawny's Wood still bothered him and he was never entirely easy with the familiarity he felt for that stretch of coastline.

The weekend was an amiable drift.

Fridays and Saturdays were changeover days when the locals were able to reclaim their territory and that, somehow, enhanced the feeling of normality. He even managed to endure a Sunday Church Service, although the sight of Batten in his gown and hood, directing operations from the choir stalls, seemed a grotesque distortion, and that made him feel weird.

It was not until Monday at tea, that his interest in the choirmaster and his operations was jump-started again.

They were eating their usual table-bound, television-free tea. Mum had only just got in from work and she said, casually, "By the way, Jack, that kid who came in just before you left – you remember him? The one who'd been injured out on the cliffs? Well, he absconded from hospital this afternoon."

"Was he okay?" Jack said. He tried to cover the missed heartbeat induced by what his mum had said. "It didn't look as if he'd ever get out of bed again, the way he was when they wheeled him in."

Mum shook her head. "He wasn't fit to leave, that's for sure. We've got the police out looking for him."

He looked at her again, and the adrenaline was coursing in his veins. "You don't do that sort of thing when a guy's bunked off, do you?"

His mum smiled enigmatically. "Sometimes we do. The police have been wanting to interview him about what happened on the cliffs. They think he was beaten up. We wouldn't let them talk to him though. He was in no way fit."

Jack dared not probe too far. It would seem suspicious if he was over-interested. All he said was, "Heck, Mum, I thought Cornwall was supposed to be a backwater. You get more excitement down here than you ever did with the criminal fraternity in Stevenage."

Mum laughed. "It's a veritable bed of vice." She sipped her glass of white wine and sat back. "But you're right.

You do get more incidents down here. It's a holiday resort; kids come down with the freedom of being unsupervised. They take on too much alcohol and they get hooked on drugs – things they'd keep more controlled when they're back in their own homes. Down here, with the lid off, they go wild and that's why they get into so much trouble."

But, by now, Jack was hardly listening. His mind was full of Greg. If he'd absconded from hospital, there would only be one place he'd head for – Three Corners' Cove and Batty Batten.

As soon as he could decently excuse himself, he made for the harbour in search of Terry.

It had been a sultry day and the sky was turning thundery. The horizon was melting into a humid grey and the sweat clung to his clothes. Along the harbour front, there was a new influx of tourists, milling around, dipping into bags of chips, swigging coke and twisting themselves into grotesque shapes to consume melting ice creams.

He could see Terry perched on the wall over by the jetty. He was exchanging the odd greeting with friends or throwing what he considered to be a seductive remark whenever he saw some girl who took his fancy among the new intake of holidaymakers. To Jack's knowledge though, his chat-up lines left vast room for improvement. Whatever he said never seemed to elicit an encouraging response.

Terry grinned when he saw him. "Got the evening off 'ave 'ee? Reward for singin' in church yesterday?"

"Yeah, and I deserve it," Jack said, clambering up onto the wall beside him. "Enduring that mental torture. I was stuck there for over an hour and seeing Batty Batten doing his thing in a church is seriously weird. It's like watching the devil dancing in the pulpit." He turned and looked at Terry. "And talking of Batten, Mum's just told me that the Greg guy's done a bunk from hospital. She said they've got the police out looking for him." He watched closely for Terry's reaction because he was anxious to pursue this. "Do you fancy taking a trip out around Three Corners' Cove in the punt?" he added. "Just to see if he's gone back there?"

Terry looked down at the thronging holidaymakers and grinned. "May as well," he said. "There isn't much talent in the intake this week."

Jack laughed. "You wouldn't get any of it, even if there was, not with your chat-up lines. I mean, 'Pretty hair you got. Natural is it, or did it come out of one of they bottles?' That isn't much of an opening gambit."

"Better chat-up line than yours," Terry said. "At least I give it a go." He scrambled down from the wall. "You say they got the police out looking for Greg?"

Jack nodded. "They wanted to interview him in hospital, but the doctors said he wasn't up to it."

"That'll be Batten," Terry said. "I reckon the police have 'ad their eye on 'im for a long time. They know 'ee's up to something, and now they've figured Greg's in it with 'im. It'll be Batten what got 'im out of hospital."

They sculled beyond the headland and then around towards Three Corners' Cove. The water was glassy. Apart from the creaking of the oar in the rowlock and the gentle splash as the boat nosed through the waves, the silence all around them was tangible.

Terry sniffed and glanced at the grey horizon. "There's going to be one hell of a storm later on," he said.

The clouds were massing and they made the feel of the evening eerie, veiled in humidity and touched with salmon pink. They were piled there, motionless, silent and other worldly, and for the first time in three days, the stillness had a stronger hint of menace about it. The woods, rambling in the ravines of the cliffside, and the cliff's undulating perimeter, seemed charged with half disclosed secrets. Even from the sea, Jack felt uneasy.

They sculled into the cove and the air was burning up. Waves hardly touched the shingle, just toppling over, stroking the shore with the faintest of movements. Not a gull stirred and the heat of the evening filled the crucible of the cove like a liquid that could be felt. It seemed to devour them as they clambered up the beach, and the scrunch of their footsteps fractured the sultry silence with brutality.

They searched every corner of the cove and behind every protrusion in the cliff, checking for signs of Greg, but there was nothing.

" 'Ee 'aven't come back 'ere," Terry said at last. "Think we should 'ave a look up on the cliff, do 'ee? See if 'ee's up there?"

The thought of climbing the cliff again, confronting the rugged inlet and the funnelling ravine, caught in Jack's gut, but, at least, if he went up there now, he'd have Terry with him. "May as well," he said. "As we've come this far."

They clambered up the rough-hewn path, groping among the promontories, and the heat had Jack's back running with perspiration. He was panting by the time they reached the top.

"You are such a wuss, simple Jack," Terry laughed. "You 'aven't got no stamina. A little climb like that and you're puffin' like a steam engine."

But Jack hardly cared.

The place, with its strident past, was probing every terminal in his brain again. He could sense the sea of bodies crawling around the cove below him, and everything was enveloped in the cloak of darkness. There was the familiar presence of men hiding behind bushes with their clubs. He could see sailing boats from another age in the still water out towards the horizon, and the whole scene was lit by the shavings of a new moon.

He looked at the ravine funnelling inland to their left.

"Where does that go?" he said.

"There's old mine-workings up there. Wheal Trennack," said Terry. "'Ee could 'ave gone up there. There don't seem to be no sign of 'im down 'ere."

It was true. There wasn't a sign of anything on the cliff, not in the present. But the shadows of the past were everywhere and Jack knew the forces were at work again.

"He could be anywhere," he said. "The cove was the most likely place and he isn't there. And it's getting dark. I don't think we'll find him, even if we do go up to the mine."

Terry shrugged. "It's your call, simple Jack. The guy's up to no good and it isn't our job to help 'im. Let 'im stew, that's what I say. Anyway, if Batten got 'im out of hospital, it's more than likely 'ee's restin' up at 'is 'ouse. You didn't think of that, did you?"

Jack gave a weak smile. It hadn't entered his head that Greg might be hiding out next-door.

But it wasn't giving up the search that made him say, "Let's go back." It was the immensity of those shadowing images on the cliff.

They scrambled down to the cove again, and the humidity was still building.

The heat and the silence bore down on them with physical force and Jack was grateful when Terry sculled out into the bay.

By the time they reached Tregenwyth, it was almost dark.

As they nosed into the harbour, the quayside was still thronging with people. Now though, the whole vista changed. The harbour wall was illuminated with chains dripping beads of coloured lights. They had festooned the jetties, reflecting in the water like multi-coloured organ pipes, and as Terry eased the punt back to its moorings, the wake set the curtain of reflections shivering. There was a buzz of life around the harbour. It was so normal, and yet, to Jack, it seemed surreal. Tonight, with the tension of the heat and the sultry intimidations, it wasn't so easy to be swallowed up by the immediacy of the quayside's activity.

They staggered up the steps, and as he emerged onto the jetty, he caught sight of Batten on the hill, climbing towards Trelawny's Wood.

"See who's on the march again," he said. "If Greg is staying at his house, the guy isn't getting much in the way of remedial attention."

Terry looked. The choirmaster was striding out in his usual way, hurrying to be on the cliff, glancing furtively over his shoulder, shifty and suspicious.

But then, something happened that made Jack grab the harbour wall for support.

As he watched Batten's progress, the cliff started to change. What was the familiar structure of the twenty-first century, began to transform itself, thrusting out tree-clad promontories that had fallen into the sea generations ago. Paths were twisting back to their ancient routes. Old trees were turning to saplings, lost trees re-appeared and new trees disappeared.

The images were swinging from the present to the past, and the striding figure of Batten changed from the neatly dressed choirmaster to his eighteenth century counterpart in white silk stockings, bright breeches, waistcoat and a flowing cloak.

"Do you want us to follow 'im?" Terry asked.

But Jack couldn't answer.

All he could do was stare at the oscillating scene. The noises of the crowd became muffled and it was as if he was suspended between the reality of the present and that picture of the past, with Batty Batten's counterpart walking the cliffs, and time wobbled.

The changes flashed on his eyes like strobe lighting and he felt sick.

"I said, do you want us to follow 'im?" Terry said again, shoving his face in front of Jack. "Are you listenin' to me or what?"

Jack pulled himself back to the present, making a superhuman effort. The power of the fluctuating scene, the hum of unreality in his head and that stultifying heat hovering over everything, seemed to be devouring him. The forces of nature and ante-nature were at war. Even Terry's face, shoved into his line of vision, appeared to be part of the nightmarish gestalt.

He shook himself. "What?"

"Bloody hell, simple Jack, where you been? You was miles away. It's only Batty Batten. You've seen 'ee often enough. Do you want for us to follow 'im? It's a chance 'ee could lead us to Greg."

Jack felt his face flushing. "Sorry," he said. "I don't know what happened. It must be the heat. It's more like the tropics. This isn't like England at all."

Terry pulled himself into a defiant stance and stared at him. "It isn't England, simple Jack. It's Cornwall. That's a different thing altogether, and don't you forget it."

Jack grinned in spite of himself. It was such a comfort to have a totally twenty-first century nationalist with both feet set firmly on the St Piran flag, standing in front of him. It took some of the sting out of it all. There was no way he could tell Terry what he was seeing though – and he could still see it – beyond Terry's superimposed head. "Sorry, Force Ten. I forgot you were one of the twenty thousand Cornishmen," he said.

"Yeah, well – you're Irish aren't 'ee? You should know about these things. Now, for the third time of askin', are you up for tracking Batten?"

There was no way though – not with time rocking like it was.

Nothing like this had ever happened before. He'd seen the odd figure, the chance instability in the hall back at the house, but this was a whole cliffside; the ramparts of roads and houses, trees and rocks; everything that made up Tregenwyth's west cliff was in ferment. It would be like walking into the lion's lair to go up there now.

"I know we've got to track the guy down," he said, shaking his head. "But…"

Terry glanced out to where the fire of the setting sun was still catching the clouds. "Yeah, you're right," he said. "We'd be up there when it's pitch black and that storm, when it do come, it would give us one hell of a soaking. It wouldn't be much fun. Best wait for another night. 'Ee do go up there all the time. After choir tomorrow? We could follow 'im then."

Jack nodded. "That would be best. Besides, if we're trying to track Greg down, like you said, he's more likely to be up at Batten's place. I mean, from what Mum told me, he wasn't fit to be scaling cliffs."

As he spoke, his eyes were still fixed on the raging instabilities. The uncertainty of it all held him transfixed.

Batty Batten was rampaging along with his eighteenth century counterpart and time, on the hillside, was rocking. It was worse than anything he'd seen before and he dreaded where it was leading. He was certain, with a whole village in ferment, something phenomenal was about to happen.

He was so glad he'd ditched the key. The very thought of going back in this turmoil made him shudder. The forces were so massive. Last time he went, he'd been stuck for nearly a fortnight and with everything rampaging with this volatile intensity… if he did go back… it might be forever.

The storm broke soon after he got home.

Heavy clouds had rolled across from the sea, and Dad had all the lights on even before the first crack of thunder.

But when the lightning came, it turned the street blue with its pyrotechnics. The flashes were like explosions. They rattled in, one after the other, lighting up everything beyond the windows and after each lightning flash came the thunder, a roll beginning with a vicious clap and then grumbling to a long fading growl around the bay.

Dad muttered something about Him upstairs moving the furniture, but none of that registered with Jack. In the blue flashes of lightning, there were things going on outside that made the thought of God moving furniture quite acceptable.

The steps and the street immediately in front of the dining room window were alive – with red-coated soldiers and carts, some trundling past, others waiting, and impatient horses stamping their hooves. Soldiers were staggering across to the carts with what looked like brandy kegs and every time the sky lit up, he could see more. There were two men, big men, with heavy greatcoats and wigs. They were being marched away from the house by some of the soldiers, and the unnatural heat in the dining room was stifling.

He couldn't move.

There were paths of electricity dancing on the railings outside and the whole scene had him riveted.

As he stared, a sudden crack of thunder burst right overhead – a sharp whip that sent rolling echoes out into the bay and the lights went out.

Dad groped in the dresser for matches and candles, but with the darkness, the visions in the street were even clearer. The shocks of lightning seemed to be coming without a break, and Jack could feel the hair on the nape of his neck rising.

He heard Dad say: "Who's for going out the back to wash up?" And he was vaguely aware of a soft flickering as he lit the candles. Even without the key, this was terrifying, and the fact that his parents were completely oblivious to what was going on outside made it worse.

Mum said, "We'll all muck in. You don't mind, do you, Jack?"

In a way he was glad. He'd give anything to get out of the dining room. In the kitchen, he wouldn't be able to see this crazy eighteenth century mummery.

"Dad can wash. We'll dry," Mum said.

They took the plates, fumbling down the passage, and Dad scraped the leftovers onto a piece of newspaper. They'd had mackerel for supper – fish that Terry had caught earlier, before Jack met up with him.

Dad folded the paper and glanced out into the backyard.

By now, the rain was adding to the pandemonium – rods of it, rattling to the ground, a roar of primeval wrath, unrelenting and exploding on the yard's surface.

He turned to Jack, shoving the folded paper in his direction. "Here, Jack, old son. You take this out. Dump it in the dustbin for me, will you?"

Jack stared as yet more lightning stuttered around the window. "I'll get soaked," he said.

"Whoever goes out will get soaked." His dad took a raincoat from a hook on the pantry door. "Drape this over your head. You'll be out there and back within seconds, and if you do get a bit wet, your skin's younger than mine. Besides, you're a faster mover. You'll be more capable of dodging the rain drops."

He began to run water into the sink and Mum was chuckling.

"For Goodness' sake, Jack, get out there. There's no way your dad will go. You know what he's like with thunder."

Jack gazed into the yard again. It was like a cauldron out there, with rain bouncing off the ground, lashing in a continuous fury... but... it was only rain. There nothing there that could compare with the mayhem going on at the front of the house, and he'd only be out for a few seconds. Besides, now he'd got rid of the key, there was no reason to be afraid.

He took the paper and made for the door.

But as soon as he was outside, he could feel it.

The air was burning up and with every flash of lightning, white-blue streaks exploded on his eyes.

The door slammed and now that he was in the yard, he knew that nothing about it was right.

There was a pump, and the rain was dancing on unfamiliar cobbles. The algae-stained concrete that he knew so well had gone. This yard wasn't the yard of the twenty-first century.

In panic, he turned towards the kitchen again, but as soon as he pushed at the door, he was certain. The door was fixed, immoveable, and naked fear took hold of him.

This time it was worse. With the door jammed, he couldn't go back to his own time... and... with no key, he couldn't complete the journey into the past.

He was stuck in some terrible no man's land and he didn't know what to do.

Then he turned as another flash of lightning ripped at the sky and for a second, he saw the back wall. There was no honeysuckle and no clematis. The wall was bare, rain-soaked and sheer, a cliff of shale and granite reaching to the electric blue heavens, and lying among the cobbles at the wall's base, glinting as the rain hissed around it, was the key he'd thrown away last week.

He didn't have to think twice.

With one bound, he leapt across the yard and grabbed it. Then he pushed it into the lock.

It was better to go back completely than be stuck here forever between times, and desperately, he shoved at the kitchen door.

18

The moonlight was cold and Jax stood shivering in the yard.

She stared around her, filling her lungs with the sharp air, grasping for courage. This would be the last time she'd make the journey onto the cliffs. After tonight, she would never play ghost for the people of Tregenwyth again, although, tonight wasn't like the other nights. She wasn't doing it for Mr Trelawny and his friends. There would be no boats to charm and no spotsmen and clubmen lurking on the cliffs. When the customs men had left after their raid last week, they'd taken the Squire and Mr Trelawny with them. They were locked up in Bodmin Jail. They hadn't taken Mr Baldwyn because no one had been able to find him. When he'd fired the pistol, he didn't aim at anyone. He just fired into the air, and after the smoke had cleared, he was nowhere to be seen.

The customs men thought he'd escaped down into the cavern, but they couldn't find any trace of him. It was as if he'd vanished into thin air.

They did find brandy though – barrels of it, stacked around the ledges in the cavern and they impounded it, much to the fury of the Tregenwyth men.

She knew all this because this afternoon, she'd been to Polgarthen.

During the raid they'd been busy with the brandy kegs, loading them onto carts, and they hadn't seemed to bother about her. When it was all over, they went away and she was left with Mrs Spargo. Even Barney appeared to have forgotten his promise to free her. But it could be for the best. She was content to stay until they knew what was happening to the Squire and Mr Trelawny. She was in no danger. And if she stayed, she wouldn't arouse suspicion as to her part in the raid.

Mrs Spargo didn't object to her going to Polgarthen. All Mrs Spargo did since Mr Trelawny had been taken away, was wander around the house wringing her hands, wondering what was to become of her.

Jax had hoped to see her brother in town, but he wasn't there. She'd hung around just so she could find out what was going on. She tried to gather as much from the talk around the market as she could. And what she heard scared her.

The customs' men, she learned, had taken the brandy to a new engine house up behind the smugglers' cove. They'd just finished building it for the Trennack Mining Company and the excise were storing the brandy there until they could move it to Gweek. There was an old front half of a boat up there. It was part of a ship that the Revenue had confiscated from a local fisherman. They sawed the boats in half when they impounded them, so the fishermen couldn't use them again. The labourers who'd been building the engine house had turned the bow of the boat into a hut – 'Three Corners Hut', they called it, and now it was being used as sleeping quarters by the dragoon who was guarding the brandy.

The Tregenwyth men planned to go up to the mine tonight. They were going to get their brandy back and they were going to torch everything that was up there – the mine, the engine house, the hut. They were planning to burn the boy as well – the one who was guarding the contraband. That way there would be nothing left to suggest what they'd done and no one to peach on them.

When she heard who the boy was, she was very frightened. They said the dragoon who was up there was the one who'd found the trap in Trelawny's cellar, and he deserved to die for that.

It was Barney who'd discovered the trap, and straightaway, she knew what she had to do. She had to go up to the mine and warn him. She had to get him away before the Tregenwyth men got to him, and the only way to do that was by going up over the cliff, using the same route as she'd used on all the other nights. She was going to dress as the ghost and sing the song, just as she always did, because then, she hoped, the rabble might hear her and begin to believe in their own myth. That would scare them away and give her and Barney time to escape.

She closed the kitchen door quietly, so as not to disturb Mrs Spargo. She'd been to Mr Trelawny's bureau in the drawing room and she'd taken the white cloak, and now she pulled it around her.

Then she made her way down the hill towards the harbour.

A cloud had obliterated the moon and it was inky black down there. The rigging on the masts and spars of the boats were rattling like a leafless forest. As she groped her way across the quay, she could hear the sound carrying across the water and its eerie clamour scared her.

For a moment she stood, filling her lungs with the salt air and then, to boost her courage, she began to sing.

"Ow huv-kolon gwra dos. A ny glewydh y'n koos,
An eos ow kana pur hweg?"

The words echoed against the bare-walled limekilns and the fishermen's lofts. But, instead of making her more courageous, her own singing filled her with terror. She persisted though, struggling up the steep cliff path to the woods, and when she reached the summit, she stood for a moment, eyeing the sea. The clouds had cleared now and she stared at the water, a vast surging expanse, glinting, stretching away in the faint light of the waning moon. And all around her were trees casting gnarled shadows, creeping like hour hands across the cliffside, and the stillness was breathless.

She pulled herself forward into the woods and began to sing again, more loudly this time.

"Akordys ens i a dhemedhi devri,
Ha distowgh dhe'n eglos dhe vos."

At last, she reached the head of the cove where the path turned inland. She knew where the three corners hut was. She'd asked Mrs Spargo where they were storing the brandy.

Since Mr Trelawny had been taken away, Mrs Spargo seemed to see her as a kindred soul in abandonment and she found consolation in having her there. She told her anything she wanted to know and she let her do much as she pleased.

Jax followed the path as Mrs Spargo had described it, climbing inland, and it wasn't long before she began to near the top of the valley where the path dog-legged towards the hill's summit.

She sang clearly, with the sound rebounding into the night, and she clung desperately to the hope that it would scare the Tregenwyth men away.

> *"A ny glewydh hy lev, a woles a sev*
> *Y'n nansow ow kana mar deg."*

As she pressed forward, she could make out the contours of the new mine on the skyline and tucked into its shadow, the weird, boat-shaped hut. That was where Barney was living. She stood for a moment and waited, hoping he would be outside, but there was no sign of movement. Either he wasn't around or he hadn't heard her, so she began to sing again:

> *"Ow huv-kolon gwra dos. A ny glewydh y'n koos."*

At last, a door in the wall of the hut swung open, and her brother emerged, standing there, tall in his dragoon's uniform, peering into the darkness.

"Martha, is that you down there?" he called, and she moved into clear view and began running towards the upturned boat.

"What you doin' up here this time of night?" he hissed.

She rested against the hut's bow, giving herself time to breathe. Then she looked hard into Barney's face. She took a deep breath and whispered, "I had to come, Barney. I had to warn you about what's goin' on down there. I was in Polgarthen today, because I was hopin' to find you, and I 'eard the talk around town. They know about you bein' up here and the brandy bein' stored in the engine house. They're goin' to raid the place tonight. They're goin' to get their brandy back and they said they're goin' to burn everything down. They're plannin' to burn you, too."

She saw Barney's hand move towards his sword and in the faint light of the moon, she could sense his face hardening. "They'd better not try," he said. "I'll take on any man that dares."

"There's scores of them," she whispered. "They're plannin' to destroy everything up here."

He didn't move for a moment, but she could sense his muscles tightening. "I aren't afraid," he said at last. But his mouth was twitching and his fingers played nervously on the hilt of his sword.

Then as they stood, searching the headland for signs of movement, she heard a crack like the burning of a dry twig just behind the engine house, and Barney swung around. "Quick," he whispered. "Get out of sight by the other side of that hut. And when they start comin', you run down that hill like the wind. If they catch sight of you, they'll kill you for certain."

His eyes were darting in all directions, searching among the shadows; but Jax' didn't move. "I aren't goin' to hide behind nothing," she said at last. "If those men are comin', I'm stayin' here with you. If they kill you, they can kill me too. I don't care. There won't be no point in me goin' on livin'; not if you're dead."

She grabbed at Barney's arm. He was drawing his sword and she could feel his body, tense with the threat, and his eyes were striving to penetrate the darkness...But then, as she stood there, shoulder to shoulder with her brother, she felt the thing inside her. It had invaded her body in the yard just before she'd left the house. She'd known it was there. She'd felt that dizzy feeling as it crept into her, and now it was fighting her again. No matter what she wanted, it was clear this creature did not want to stay with Barney and before she could stop it, it had her out of control and she was running down the hill. Not only was she running, but she was screaming at the top of her voice: "Mum! – Dad! – Get me out of here! – Quick! – Save me!"

The words made no sense. They weren't part of her, but, as soon as the Tregenwyth men heard the voice, the whole place burst into life. Shadows leapt from behind trees and rocks. Men swarmed from nowhere, waving clubs and yelling. Someone took a dive at her feet and as she fell, she heard a man shout from just behind her, "I know who she is. That's Trelawny's maid."

Barney made a lunge to save her. But as he moved, they grabbed him, and one of the villagers launched into him with a club, landing a blow across his head that must have split his skull.

She wanted to reach out for him, but the man who'd brought her down was straddling her, holding her to the ground and he was shouting, his voice vicious with malice. "This must be the bitch who blabbed to the Revenue. She's up 'ere with that dragoon. She'll be 'is fancy woman more than like."

He shook her, making her look into his face, and his features were twisted with rage. "You're nothin but a little trollop," he snarled. "Too free with yer tongue was 'ee, in the soldier boy's bed?" Then he hit her across the face and the blow nearly knocked her senseless.

"Tie she up and leave she to burn with 'im," someone called from up by the engine house, and she could feel rough hands gripping her, lashing her with rope, while, all the time, the thing inside her was screaming, "Mum! Dad! I'm going to die. Get me back. Save me!"

They were pulling her towards the hut now and they were dragging Barney too.

When they got them up to the engine house, they left her bound and helpless, while all around, pandemonium raged.

She could make out the black silhouettes of men gathering brushwood. They were stacking it by the mine and laying a trail in her direction. Then, with a cry of jubilation, someone struck a flint and flames began to lick around the engine house wall. Acrid smoke filled the air, drifting towards her and her brother, and through the shimmering haze she could see the Tregenwyth men with their faces blackened, dancing and rolling the brandy kegs down the hill.

She struggled desperately, the rope burning into her wrists, and slowly, the heat around her grew more intense.

And all the time she was yelling in confused terror, "Barney, get me out of here. Mum!...Dad!...I'm dying!"

The flames were creeping nearer and the heat shimmered over the grasses. She screamed again, rolling herself to be nearer the lifeless body of her brother, while everywhere, terror and confusion raged.

The spirit-thing inside her was calling for her father and that was a treacherous, wicked thing to do because she knew her father was dead.

Then, with a crack of thunder and a vicious dart of lightning, she heard the kitchen door bursting open and dad was there, bending over an inert body.

...And out of the confusion, Jack heard the gentle voice of his father saying, "Are you all right, son? Are you okay?"

He turned towards him, his eyes blank, with the rain and tears pouring down his face, and he sobbed, "Barney! Barney!"

He was still between times and all the horror of the night was shuddering through him.

Then he collapsed into his father's arms, still sobbing out the name of the boy.

"Barney," he cried. "My brother, Barney ...Barney."

19

There were a lot more questions this time.

Who was Barney? And he'd called him 'brother'. What brother? What had happened to him out there?

His dad wanted to know if he'd been struck by lightning and his mum checked him over.

"It looks like a re-occurrence of that spasm last week, when we had him in hospital," she said. "There's no sign of anything wrong externally. He's as fit as a flea, and there'll be nothing internal. We've tested everything."

She wiped the rain from his face. "So – what happened Jack? Do you think you were fitting out there? Was it the thunder? Did that scare you?"

He shook his head.

All these questions; it was adding to his confusion, and he couldn't cope with his mother's interrogations. He couldn't even jibe at her for asking him about fitting – as if he'd know!

His head was full of contradictions and this time, the sense of death and unfathomable grief was seared into every membrane of his body.

Who *was* Barney? And who was the other person who'd felt the scorching heat? Because there *was* another person. Up until now, he'd always imagined he'd been the one that was back there. But the person who'd felt the heat wasn't him. He wasn't even sure it had been him out in the yard. It certainly wasn't him calling for Barney.

Someone had been calling though, from inside him, and that someone was so close to being him, it was his voice that had called the name.

Back in the other time, he thought there was someone, and somehow that someone's life was bound up with his so that when he went back, he became part of that other person...and he felt that the force binding them was stronger than any human bond.

He could still feel, deep inside him, the grief for Barney, and it wasn't a 'manly' grief. He began to sense it was a girl he inhabited. This was the death-grieving of a sister for a brother.

And the sense of death was absolute – raging fires and darkened figures, and these fires hadn't happened in the back yard. The burning had been in some place away from the house, some downland on the cliff.

He struggled to bring himself to the realisation that he was Jack O'Hagan, citizen of the twenty-first century. But the emotional ties to Barney remained as real and as strong as anything in the present.

He was also beginning to realise that it had been Barney he'd remembered from the cellar – the young soldier by the trap door, and it was Barney on the cliff being attacked by those men with their clubs. And all this he'd seen through the eyes of Barney's sister. She had somehow melded with him, filling his soul. It wasn't just her brother who was dying either – the girl who he'd become part of – she was dying too, and the grief and the loss inside him was something more massive than anything he'd ever felt.

He didn't know how to deal with it, and his mum's probings and his dad's anxieties were intrusions. He just couldn't cope with them.

"You must remember, Jack, old son," his dad was saying. "You were shouting some boy's name. Barney. Now where did that come from? And...calling him your brother...is it some fantasy – because you're an only child? Have you had to invent an imaginary sibling? Is it our fault for not giving you a brother or sister? Would that be it?"

It was such a ridiculous concept that if Jack wasn't so eaten up with pain, he would have laughed. "It hasn't got anything to do with any siblings," he muttered. "Believe me, it's bad enough having to live with you two sometimes, without having to put up with a product of your combined genetic mutations."

Mum sniffed. "Well, thanks for that, Jack," she said.

In spite of himself, he smiled. "That didn't come out right. What I meant was, you can have too much of a good thing."

"So you don't mind being an only child?" his dad said.

He shrugged. "Never gave it much thought, to be honest."

"It still doesn't explain this Barney you were shouting for," Mum said. "We're still none the wiser as to what happened out there."

He pulled his knees up to his chest and clasped them with his hands. Moving was uncomfortable because his clothes were soaking wet. Everything he was wearing clung to his skin.

But there was no point in hiding it any more. Even if they didn't get it, he was going to tell them. "It's only been happening since we came down here," he said.

"We know that," said Mum.

"And what I'm going to tell you is so weird, you're not going to believe any of it."

Dad looked at him closely. "Go on, son."

"Well, since we've been here it's like I know this place. Like I've been here before, and sometimes, just now for instance, and when you carted me off to hospital, it's as if I'm not here in the present. It's like I go off into a different age. I mean, something must have happened here in the past and…I go into another time zone or something, and I sort of experience what happened back there."

"And what does happen?" his dad said and Jack couldn't be sure whether his father was humouring him or if he was genuinely interested.

"That's the trouble," he said. "I don't know. It's like, when I come back, I can't remember anything, only vague feelings. But there's something bad going on back there and I'm sure Barney is there, and some other person – Barney's sister, I think, but I can't be certain."

He noticed glances passing between his parents and his mum frowned. "That's a strange story, Jack," she said. "It must be some nightmare. That's why you can't remember it when you wake up. There's something about this place that's got under your skin. It's playing on your mind."

He shrugged. He knew it was going to be hopeless. They wouldn't believe him. Already, his mum was diluting his experiences into the trivialities of nightmares. There was no point in reminding them that the very first day, he'd known the door under the stairs led to a cellar. And how could he have had a nightmare out in the yard when he'd only been there for a few seconds?

Mum stood up and levered him into a standing position. "Have we used all the hot water?" she said, looking at Dad.

His father shook his head. "There'll be plenty."

"Then I suggest, Jack, you take a candle, go up to the bathroom, and have a good hot soak," his mum said. "Then get into some dry clothes. You'll feel a lot better after a soak and when you've got something warm and dry on."

The soak in a candle-lit bathroom should have been the perfect antidote to his backyard experiences, but, this time, nothing could shift the trauma.

He'd touched the face of death and the only things occupying him were a sense of darkness, the fire encroaching from all directions and the abrasion of scorching heat. He could feel the searing pain of it even now.

After the bath, he went down to join his parents in the lounge, but it was as if he was no longer part of this world. His mind was in the fog of confusion and in spirit, he felt as though he was trapped between the centuries.

Even when the storm had died down and the electricity was back on, he still couldn't drag himself into the present, and that night, he hardly slept.

Next morning, the subtropical air that had given them the unrelenting heat had gone.

Jack looked from his bedroom window and saw a sky crisp and brisk with white clouds, and there was a sharper, colder mood to everything.

It wasn't conducive to relaxation and a heavy feeling of grief stayed with him all morning.

He didn't get up in spite of his dad's cajoling.

There seemed to be no impetus to face the day, and Dad's urgings from the bottom of the stairs did lack passion. The events of the previous evening must have been at the back of his mind too.

After lunch, he ambled down to the harbour and the whole place had a different feel to it.

The sea was ribbed with sharp tipped waves. They were white-topped where the lips curled and the blue of the water was inky. A chilling breeze whipped across the bay, and somehow, even though the sun was beating down, the holidaymakers had sharpened up their movements. There was more purpose and there was a smattering of bright plastic Macs where there'd been chilled-out T-shirts before.

Terry was on the wall people-watching. He'd sorted out his lines for the day and he was ready to go fishing, but for Jack, a trip out into the bay had lost its appeal. There wasn't the calm indolence out there anymore, and besides, his enthusiasm for any kind of activity had been dulled by this ambiguous grieving.

"I said it would be bad last night," Terry said.

"Dad made me go out into the yard to dump the fish bones," said Jack as he clambered onto the wall beside him. "I was only out there for a few seconds and I was drenched."

"Good, though, wasn't it?" said Terry. "I reckon you could 'ave read a book in that lightning."

Jack didn't answer. In that lightning, you could have done a lot of things and he had – unspeakable things that he couldn't shake from his mind.

They watched the fluctuations of the crowds and Terry managed to get the attention of a group of girls.

They congregated at the foot of the wall, laughing and exchanging trivialities. But somehow, the girls' attitude made Jack feel patronised. It was clear they found Terry's rugged looks and Latin complexion appealing; but their interest in red-headed Jack, Terry's freckled companion, bordered on the indifferent.

It was while the girls were crowding around with their inane giggles and banter that he saw something and it galvanized him out of his indolence. Skulking among the crowds on the other side of the jetty and easing gingerly between the hordes, he suddenly saw Greg. He was edging towards the west cliff, his left arm in a rag of a sling and his face scarred and bruised. As he broke free from the crowds, Jack could see he was walking with a marked limp. But his intention was clear. He was heading for Trelawny's Wood and the cliff.

Jack nudged Terry who was waxing eloquent for the benefit of his captive audience, although his repartee was failing to rise above what they expected. It was still the inane droolings of the local 'rough'. He looked up when Jack nudged him.

"What's the trouble?" he asked, and Jack nodded towards the western perimeter of the harbour.

"You can see what the trouble is. And he hasn't got his side-kick with him either."

Terry whistled softly. "Go after 'im, shall we?"

"Seems like a plan," Jack said. "He's so crocked, he'll be easy to follow."

It was a wrench for Terry. He'd been in full cry and he looked down at his bunch of acolytes. "We got to go," he said. "But you're down 'ere all week aren't 'ee? I'll be 'ere most days. We can meet up again tomorrow if you like."

"Yeah, sure," one of the girls said. "You going to take us out in your little boat, then?"

"I can, if you want," Terry said. "Me and Jack, we do go out most days."

The thought of five giggling teenagers crowding on top of him in that punt, preening themselves for Terry's attentions, made Jack shudder…but there might be something in it for him. There was one girl he'd noticed, smaller than the rest and quieter, and she'd been glancing in his direction. She was less brash than the others. He'd been giving her the occasional smile and she hadn't seemed averse to his attentions. Terry didn't go any further than hinting at a bit of fishing, which was a relief. He could have gone on to invite them to Three Corners' Cove for a spot of skinny-dipping and that would have put the mockers on the whole excursion. He must be learning or he was more taken with the prospect of trailing Greg.

They slid off the wall and made for the west cliff.

When they got there, Greg was already half way up the hill, but his progress was slow, and although he was keeping an eye out for pursuers, he only turned occasionally and when he did, it was obvious he was in pain. There were no quick glances and he telegraphed his movements so clearly that Jack and Terry were able to dip into a gateway or behind a hedge whenever he turned.

Once they were on the cliff, concealing themselves was easier and their pursuit was fairly unhampered.

At one point, Greg stopped, obviously in an area where there was a strong phone signal, because he made a call on his mobile.

"That'll be to Batten," Terry whispered. "They two are as thick as thieves."

"Where do you think he's going?" said Jack.

"There've got to be some outlet to that shaft. It'll be up by Wheal Trennack more than like."

They continued their pursuit, and although Greg struggled, hampered by his makeshift sling and injured legs, there was a sense of purpose in his movements, and eventually, he made it across to Three Corners' Cove.

There the path took a sharp turn to the right, following the valley inland climbing up towards Trennack Downs.

"It's like I said. He's headin' straight for Wheal Trennack," Terry whispered.

They hung back more now. The downland was bare of scrub, and as they got further up the incline, it became clear that Greg was conscious of something behind him. He kept turning his torso; looking back, and his body language showed he was uneasy. He never saw them though, and between turns, he struggled on until they rounded a hook in the path, and there, for the first time, Jack saw the downs sweeping up to the broken ruins of the mine's engine house at Wheal Trennack. The chimney was still intact and stood proud, but the engine house walls were crumbling. Its silhouette was broken against the sharp blue of the skyline and Jack gasped. But this time it wasn't because he *felt* he'd been there before. He *knew* he'd been there and he knew everything about it.

It was the place where he'd been last night, where the fire had burned, where the dark shapes of men had swarmed, rolling barrels down towards the cliff. It was where Barney, and Jack's strange alter ego had been left to the devouring flames. It was the place of a dark night and the death that had plagued him ever since. It was where, over two centuries ago, that other part of him had been destroyed.

Terry glanced at him. He seemed confused by the terror in his eyes. "Is there something going on up there?" he whispered.

And there *was* something going on.

Etched against the sky, they saw two men, tall, bruising figures, watching Greg's progress from the ruined engine house, and they were signalling to him, pointing back down the hill.

Greg turned and it all happened too quickly. There was no time for them to hide.

"Hey, you two kids!" he yelled. He began to lope back in their direction. "You been following me or what?" He cursed and stumbled. "Batten told you to keep away from here."

They didn't waste any time. They just turned and tore towards the cliff with Terry giving a parting shot over his shoulder. "It's a free country, mister. We aren't breaking no rules."

But Greg's voice came back, "You get lost! And don't you go following me no more."

They didn't stop running. They didn't even turn to see if they were being pursued. They just legged it over the cliff, through Trelawny's Wood and down to the security of the quayside.

When they got there, Terry threw himself against the harbour wall. He was panting. "I told, 'ee, didn't I?" he gasped. "They got those men up there. Are they the ones you saw in the cavern?"

Jack could hardly speak. He was even more busted by the pell-mell retreat than Terry. At last, he said, "They could be, but it was so dark and those guys up by the mine were too far away. I couldn't be certain."

"What's goin' on up there?" Terry asked.

Jack shook his head. "I haven't a clue."

"Should we go to the police, do you think?" But Jack had thought of the police before. The trouble was, there was so much of his story that would be hard to explain – time portals and going into the past and the like.

"What have we got to tell them," he said, "other than there's something going on under Batten's cellar with foreign men and that it's connected with Wheal Trennack?"

Terry eased himself onto the wall. He had a rueful smile on his face. "I reckon you got somethin' a bit more urgent to deal with, anyway. Greg's goin' to tell Batten what we done and you got choir tonight."

Jack gulped. He'd forgotten about the choir and the thought sent a shudder right through him.

He wasn't going to miss it though. Some instinct told him the link with Batten and the choir was a vital part of all this. "He won't do anything, not with all the others there, and if he does corner me, I'll just say we saw Greg going up on the cliff all bashed up and we followed to make sure he was okay."

Terry sniffed and assisted Jack onto the wall. "Rather you than me," he said. "Because I reckon, once that guy've heard from Greg that we was on the cliff, 'ee's going to be gunnin' for us, big time."

There was a look of resolve on Jack's face. "If I don't go tonight I'll just be shelving it. It's better I face up to him at choir than in some dark street somewhere. Anyway, I'd rather do it now and get it over with. The longer you put things off, the more anxious you get."

Terry grinned. "Proper little philosopher, aren't 'ee, simple Jack. You go to choir then. And afterwards, meet me down 'ere. They girls might be around again by then and we can share a bag of chips with them."

Jack laughed, digging him in the side. "You're such an old romantic, Force Ten. That'll really turn them on – sharing a bag of chips with you."

Terry was still grinning. "All you got to do is watch and learn, simple Jack. Just watch …and learn, that's all."

20

He wasn't looking forward to going to the church hall, even though he'd shrugged the subject away when Terry had reminded him.

But nothing good would come from putting off the confrontation. Besides, his intention, last week, when he'd brought the note from Greg, was to let Batten know he wasn't intimidated by his veiled threats, and as far as the choirmaster was concerned, nothing had changed.

Even so, by the time he reached the hall, he was seriously tempted to do a runner. It was only his common sense that persuaded him retreat would be pointless.

Taking a deep breath, he stepped over the threshold and marched boldly through the door, and there was much the same activity inside as there had been the previous week. Knots of boys and men were standing around with coffee and biscuits. The younger kids were mainly on cartons of soft drink, and Batten was with Mr James at the front of the hall, discussing the music they were going to rehearse.

Jack eyed him, watching to see if there was any reaction as he walked in, but there was nothing and Jack mingled as best he could.

It wasn't a great performance. He hated socialising, especially in places where there were well-established cliques. It made him feel like an interloper, and he wasn't comfortable when the old guy who'd greeted him last week came up and started making small talk.

In spite of his belief that a confrontation with Batten was the best option, he still couldn't help feeling that being in proximity to the guy was like standing next to an unexploded bomb.

He knew so much about him. He knew he wasn't human – not in the accepted sense. He wasn't subject to the normal laws of physics. He could exist beyond the constraints of time, disappearing and then re-appearing centuries later, and everything he did reeked of corruption.

He tried not to think about it, but he was on edge with the old guy standing next to him, wanting to know was he settling in okay, and did he like living in Cornwall, and had he been in a choir before. Batten's image wouldn't move from his consciousness. He realised he was a bit curt with the old chap, but he couldn't lose the thought that standing by the keyboard at the front of the hall was some monster capable of…who knew what?

As the choir members began to drift to their places, Batten ended his discussion with Mr James and he did give Jack a glance. His flabby face seemed clouded with malice. He didn't say anything, but the vibes weren't friendly. And when the choir had settled, he left him in no doubt. Having tapped his music stand and announced that they had a busy evening ahead, he turned his icy stare on the trebles and said, "And when we've finished, O'Hagan, before you go, I would appreciate a word in your shell-like, if that's not too much of an inconvenience to you."

There were irritating giggles from the other kids and some knowing nudges. Normally, Jack would have reacted, but the shot, directed so publicly, was like a dart. He knew immediately that their excursion onto the cliff had been noted and it wasn't going to pass unchallenged.

He tried to put it to the back of his mind; he'd just face up to it when the time came, although he'd make sure Mr James was still there when the confrontation took place.

For the first part of the practice, it was hard to concentrate.

But then, something changed.

It happened when the rehearsal was drawing to its close. Batten paused and looked around. He cleared his throat, and somehow, there was an edginess about him. He settled his pig-like eyes on Jack ... and Jack felt he was mulling over the confrontation that was looming at the end of the practice.

But all he said was: "Towards Christmas, gentlemen, we will be taking part in a small festival in Polgarthen and as our contribution, I would like us to learn a new song. It's a favourite of mine, a little folk song I've known for a very long time."

He picked up a sheaf of music and his stare still burned into Jack.

There was a general shuffle and Mr James began passing out the music sheets.

Now Batten's eyes were off Jack and he was adjusting the scores on his stand. Jack couldn't understand the look he'd given him. It was intense, but it seemed to have no relevance to what was going on in the hall.

He glanced through the music. The words were simple – as Batten had said – a little folk song.

"My sweet heart come along, don't you hear the fond song.
The sweet notes of the nightingale flow.
Don't you hear the fond tale of the sweet nightingale?
As she sings in the valley below."

It seemed that Batten's mind was more pre-occupied with Jack's and Terry's excursion to Wheal Trennack, and if he was honest, that scared him. But he steeled himself and as the choirmaster tapped on his music stand again, he stared unblinkingly at the words in front of him.

"Mr James will run through the melody to familiarise you before we try it," Batten said, and Mr James settled himself at the keyboard, playing through the verse.

It was while the tune was being played that Jack felt the first slight tremor, as if some inner strength had invaded him.

Then Batten lifted his hands, and as the song filled the church hall, a shudder of electricity leapt through every nerve in his body. While the rest were singing, he heard his own voice, strong and true like an angel's, carving a line over the top of the choir:

"Ow huv-kolon gwra dos. A ny glewydh y'n koos,
An eos ow kana pur hweg?
A ny glewydh hy lev a woles a sev,
Y'n nansow ow kana mar deg?"

He had no idea what he was doing, but it wasn't long before the other voices had faded into stunned silence. Even Mr James's attempts on the keyboard had stumbled. But as Jack sang, he knew that what he was singing was deep in its significance, both for him and for Batty Batten.

There was no other sound in the hall now, and his voice was otherworldly. It was almost not his voice. But he carried on, filling the space with the most amazing sound, and as he sang, he watched Batten's face.

"Na fyll, Betty ger, na vydh yn ahwer," he sang,
"Dha gelorn y'n degav dhe'th vos."

The choirmaster was suddenly staring and his features were frozen. His baton hardly moved. It was just twitching like a fading heartbeat and Jack could see the beads of sweat rising up on his waxy face. His mouth was twisting in wordless contortions and the guy seemed to be struggling with something that was almost like fear.

After the second verse, he attempted to regain his composure, but now the whole mood had changed. He was no longer in control and Jack wondered if that was the reason for his intense stare. Did Batten, in some weird way, suspect something like this might happen? He tapped weakly on his music stand to bring Jack's singing to a halt and then he grabbed at a hanky. He was shaking as he wiped the perspiration from his forehead.

"Most impressive," he said. He attempted a smile, but it was the sickly smile of someone in trauma. "I wasn't aware that you were cognisant of the Cornish language, Mr O'Hagan."

That made Jack start.

"I'm not," he said.

Batten wiped his face again because grease and sweat were still oozing from his pores. "Well, you may take my word for it, boy. What you have just sung was in perfect Cornish."

He put his baton down and the rest of the choir stared at Jack. He could have done without that kind of high profile attention, but he hadn't been able to stop himself. He had no idea what had made him sing the song in Cornish.

The effect on the choirmaster was amazing. The menace and threat in him had wilted into a wild, animal fear. He stared around the hall and then, in a voice that was forced and struggling for composure, he said, "I can't see how we can follow that, do you, gentlemen? I suggest we bring our activities to a conclusion and let O'Hagan's rendition reverberate in our ears until our next practice."

Then he made for the door, calling over his shoulder for Mr James to lock up.

As soon as he'd gone, Jack was surrounded, especially by the younger members of the choir. They wanted to know how he'd done it; what it was all about; why it had sent Batty Batten out into the village like an Exocet.

Some of their questions he didn't know the answer to, others he found hard to explain, and anyway, there was an urgent compulsion in him to get away from the hall and chase after Batten. Something told him that, at last, he had the advantage and he must act on it without delay.

He had no idea what had made him sing and the fact that he could do it at all freaked him out; but he'd been dealing with things that had been freaking him out ever since he'd arrived in Tregenwyth – Batten, his trips into the past and the fact that in another time period, he inhabited someone else's body and experienced someone else's life; all of these things were packed with the freak-out factor. The singing was just another in a long list, but this time it had scared the daylights out of the choirmaster.

He shook his head and shrugged at his interrogators. "Don't know," he said. "I haven't a clue why I sang in Cornish, nor why it freaked Batten out, but if it's not putting you at too much of an inconvenience, I'm getting out of here so I can find out."

The old man who'd been trying to befriend him called after him: "You be careful with that Mr Batten, young man. He's got a nasty streak in him. You make sure you don't get into any trouble."

"Don't worry, I'll make sure," Jack shouted, and then he burst into the street, tearing down the hill to the jetty where he found Terry waiting on the harbour wall.

"'Aven't seen they girls yet," Terry said as he came racing up to him. "So there isn't no need to rush down 'ere like a greyhound after a rabbit. You 'aven't missed nothing."

But Jack had other things on his mind. "Batten," he gasped. "Have you seen him?" And immediately, Terry's expression changed.

"After you, is 'ee? Did Greg tell 'im we was up on they cliffs this afternoon?"

"I think so, but that isn't what's going on now. Everything's changed. I've got him on the run."

"*You* 'ave?" Terry said. "'Ow come you managed that?"

"It's a long story and it's, well, weird. But have you seen him?"

Terry shook his head. "'Ee 'aven't come down 'ere. I thought 'ee was up at the church hall doin' 'is practice."

"He was, but something happened and he did a runner. We've got to go up on the cliff. He'll be up there somewhere."

"Are you plannin' to take 'im on then?" Terry said.

Jack shrugged and looked slightly bemused. He was doing all this on instinct. There was no plan. "I don't know," he said. "All I know is we've got to follow him…and you've got to be prepared for something not right to happen."

Terry eased himself off the wall. He was looking very bewildered. "I can't make 'ead nor tail of what you're saying," he said. "You sure you aren't on something?"

Jack laughed. "No. But I might as well be the mind-blowing thing that's just happened."

"Well, are you going to tell me?"

"No time. We have to get up on those cliffs, but you've got to trust me, Force Ten. I know what I'm doing, and I'm really sure weird things are going to happen up there."

Terry gave an uneasy laugh. "In Trelawny's Wood? This time o' night? Weird things are bound to 'appen."

There was a tension as he spoke and Jack sensed he wasn't completely comfortable with the prospect.

He could see time was warping the headland again, just as it had last night, but this time he wasn't afraid.

They reached the cliff path that ran along the headland, and all the time, Jack searched the gloom, anxious to catch a glimpse of the choirmaster or his eighteenth century counterpart. But there was nothing.

Yet…something was happening…an agitation between the trees down towards the cliff edge. Terry was the first to notice. All of a sudden, he looked at Jack, his eyes wide and, if it was possible, his gelled hair, done up in anticipation of sharing a bag of chips with his nearly-conquests, would have stood up even more than it already did. "Can you 'ear that?" he whispered.

Jack stood still and listened…and he *could* hear it; it was a sound that ripped through him, sending shivers down his spine.

"Ow huv-kolon gwra dos, A ny glewydh y'n koos…"

It was just as he'd sung it in the church hall, the same song, the same words, but now it wasn't coming from him. It was coming from somewhere down beyond the cliff.

"It's that ruddy ghost," Terry hissed. "And I tell you what, simple Jack, I'm gettin' out of 'ere."

Jack grabbed him. It had shaken him too, but after the last month of paranormal bombardments and with the singing in the church hall still fresh in his head, he wasn't scared. It was almost excitement. He needed Terry with him though. "Stay with me Force Ten," he whispered. "You've got to remember what I told you. I said weird things were going to happen, and everything's tied up with Batten. There's more to that guy than you know about."

Terry didn't say anything. He was gripping Jack's arm and there was sweat glistening on his face, and as he stood there, rooted in fear, the song grew louder.

"Na fyll, Betty ger, na vydh yn ahwer
Dha gelorn y'n degav dhe'th vos."

Neither of them moved. They just gazed into the darkening mass of Trelawny's Wood and then, glimpsing beyond the cliff, Jack saw it – something white, suspended in the air. It was appearing and disappearing and it seemed to be passing behind objects…objects that weren't there anymore – trees and obstacles from the past. The thing was walking on a cliff that had eroded into the sea years ago and as it came nearer, even Jack was transfixed. It was this white thing that was singing, and slowly, it moved from the non-existent cliffs and pathways to the paths that had been trodden by Jack and Terry. Then it looked up, focusing directly into Jack's eyes…and he gasped.

He knew that face. He'd seen it before, reflected back at him from a brass panel on the attic door at home.

"That's Martha," he whispered. "That's Martha Jax." He was struggling to reconcile the torrent of confusion and amazement in his head; the pieces of the jigsaw were coming together. This face that was looking up at him, this slight figure in white – translucent and as ephemeral as a mist in the air…was his other self…the host to his spirit in the eighteenth century and he couldn't control his tongue. He just gasped out: "That's me down there!"

Terry was rigid. His grip on Jack's arm was so tight, it was hurting. He didn't seem to hear what Jack had said. He just watched as the spectral shape looked up. But now, Jack was remembering whole chunks of the past. Martha Jax had sung that song, walking the cliffs on cold autumn nights, dressed in a white shift and in some remarkable way, Martha Jax was part of him.

She'd stopped singing and she stared for a few seconds. Then she turned, moving towards Three Corners' Cove. And to Jack, it was as if all the forces against Batten were amassing; him singing the Cornish song, wrong-footing the choirmaster in the church hall, sending him scurrying out onto the cliff, his unnatural urge to pursue the guy and now this sudden appearance of his soul-host from the eighteenth century – and both of them had it in mind to head towards Three Corners' Cove and Wheal Trennack. It all pointed to the same thing; the powers were conspiring against a timeless pursuer of evil.

"We've got to follow her," he whispered.

But Terry wouldn't budge. At last, he found his voice and gulped: "You follow what you like, mate, but if that thing's goin' some place, then I'm goin' some place else."

"Look, Force Ten," Jack was still whispering – anything louder would have been an intrusion. "She isn't going to hurt us. I'd stake my life on it. Don't ask me how, but I know. She's here to support us. I told you things were going to get weird. If you stick with me, you'll be all right, but you've got to stay with me."

Terry didn't utter another word, but he nodded and gulped again. He was still gripping Jack's arm and slowly, he dragged one foot after the other in the direction of Three Corners' Cove.

Jax floated ahead of them and apart from the sea's swell breaking its rhythm onto the rocks below, there was no sound, – not even the cry of an occasional gull.

When she reached the cove, she turned, taking the path up the hill. As Jack suspected, she was making for Wheal Trennack. They followed and once again, he knew the feel of the place. He'd made this journey before, only then he'd been in the body of Martha Jax and he had the certain belief that on that occasion, it had been for her, a march to the death.

They headed towards the hilltop and around the ridge, exposing the ruins of Wheal Trennack. And again, as he saw it, the first images that hit his mind were from the other age. He saw the engine house, newly built, and there was a hut made out of an upturned boat's bow. There were blackened faces. He saw his soul-host, Martha Jax, tied up by the hut and a boy, lying bleeding beside her, and he saw the flames of a brushwood fire raging towards their inert bodies.

The image melted into the present and the sharp-edged contours of the engine house crumbled into the familiar ruins as Jax moved towards it.

She was travelling more slowly now and Jack was aware of the momentous weight of all this. It was the moment when everything about the last tortuous month would either implode, leaving devastation all around him or it would explode, shattering Batten's twenty-first century operation once and for all, and he could feel his heart racing.

He knew they must tread warily, but then he heard voices. They were raised and very familiar. He could hear the African voices he'd heard in the cavern under Batten's house, and there was Greg's voice screaming something, and then he heard Batten, harsh and vicious, yelling in the African dialect.

Jax didn't deviate from her course. She rounded the engine house wall, but she was slowing down and then she stopped altogether. It was a moment of awesome thrill for Jack because she beckoned him and Terry with her right arm and it was the first time she'd communicated with him directly.

"Come on," he whispered, pulling Terry towards the engine house.

Terry's eyes were still glazed and he was as white as paper. He followed Jack, not saying a word until they reached the periphery of the ruined building.

They were standing in front of Jax now and they stared at the mayhem inside the ruins. There were about twelve

Africans, and scattered around the tumbling walls were sleeping bags and detritus suggesting months of habitation. There was an old, battered Volkswagen camper van parked by the side of the mine and it looked as if someone had been loading it, ready for an immediate departure. Greg was wrestling with one of the men, an old guy with greying hair. Jack could see his eyes wide with fury and Greg was kicking him, swearing, raining punches on him, yelling at him that no way were they leaving without him and Batten.

It was pandemonium and it was as if after Jack's song, Batten was hell-bent on getting away with all his crew, while the others wanted to leave without him and Greg.

He was certain they'd stumbled on something profoundly bad. Batten had a piece of wood and he was threatening with it, holding it like a club, driving the other men into a corner and Jack didn't know what to do. He'd come up here, full of bravado, ready to do battle, and now, in this chaos, he felt helpless.

But suddenly, as he stood there with Terry gripping his arm, he experienced the most awesome sensation.

Jax had moved slowly towards him, and for a few seconds, she floated right through him...and while the two of them were together, every degree of warmth was frozen out of him. It was as if his whole being was plunged into the cold of absolute zero – frozen into the ice of time and space, and for those few seconds, he knew and felt everything that Martha Jax knew and felt. Her emotions at seeing Batten were channelled right through him and there was a deep and profound loathing and a desire to destroy every corruption he stood for.

The moment passed and her white figure drifted to the other side of the stack. Then she rose slightly, so that she was hovering above the choirmaster and suddenly, she began to sing again:

"Ow huv-kolon gwra dos. A ny glewydh y'n koos,
An eos ow kana pur hweg?"

The words echoed off the walls in the voice of a disembodied soul and Batten leapt around, dropping the stick, and his eyes were blind with terror.

Jack was rigid. He still hadn't got over the shock of melding so utterly with Jax' spirit, but then, as if driven by a force that was outside himself, he began singing too, the same words in the same voice, and between them, they filled the ruins with a sound that made the stones tremble:

"Na fyll, Betty ger, na vydh yn ahwer,
Dha gelorn y'n degav dhe'th vos."

It was primeval. Terry was standing on the edge of the ruined engine house stunned to petrifaction. But the effect on Batten was absolute. He covered his ears, while his eyes darted from Jack to Jax and back again. Greg and the Africans were frozen to the spots where they stood, and their eyes gleamed with terror.

It was as if the whole weight of the elements was bombarding the ancient engine house walls, ringing in the stones with the penetration of laser power.

Then with an ear-splitting scream, Batten rushed out of the mine and tore non-stop down the valley, dashing out towards the cliff.

Terry swung around, moving away too and either in pursuit of Batten, or scared witless, he broke into a run.

Jax floated to the top of the wall and remained there. She was silent again now, but she was watching over the cowering Africans and Greg.

For a few moments, Jack didn't move. He was uncertain what to do. Then he was running down towards the cliff with the figure of Batten etched ahead of him.

...But even as he ran, he knew.

Batten would reach the cliff edge and he wouldn't turn. Nor would he stop. He'd just take a leap into the abyss. He'd appear for one moment, suspended in the air like a grotesque crucifix and then...he'd be gone.

He'd done it before in the cellar of Jax' house, over two hundred years ago, and he'd do it again now.

21

Although he knew what to expect, it still rocked Jack's senses and there was no way Terry was expecting it. He wasn't expecting anything that had happened since they'd set off for the cliffs, and when Jack arrived, he was just staring, his face drained, registering horror and confusion.

"'Ee's gone over," he whispered. "Straight over. 'Ee never even tried to stop. 'Ee got there before I could get to 'im."

"I know," Jack said. He was panting from the race down the hill. "I knew he'd do that."

Terry turned to him and frowned with an expression of bewilderment. "'Ow come? It's like none of this is a surprise to you."

Jack touched his arm; "There's a lot I've got to tell you, Force Ten. I've been living with these things since the day I came to Tregenwyth."

"What do you mean, living with these things? Ghosts and that weird song? I mean, it's like you knew that song as well as she did and no way was it in English. It was more like an ancient chant."

"It was Cornish," Jack said.

"Well 'ow come you know Cornish?"

Jack shrugged. "I don't. I just knew that song."

"It don't make no sense," Terry muttered. "It's like, I'm in this nightmare. And what the hell are we goin' to do about Batten and those Africans up Wheal Trennack?"

Jack took a step towards the cliff. His stomach was lurching and Terry grabbed him. "You don't want to look over there," he said. "Batten's body will be splashed out all over they rocks. It won't be no pretty sight. I tell you, it's finished me for goin' skinny dipping down Three Corners' Cove."

"There won't be anything down there," Jack said. He moved towards the edge again and common sense screamed that the statement he'd just made was nonsense. But it was his gut feeling. He really believed Batten's body wouldn't be there.

He peered over, almost afraid to take in what he might see, but…he was right. There was nothing. The rocks and chasms were unsullied, and apart from the usual debris and seaweed, the beach was empty. "See?" he said, pulling Terry towards the edge. "It's like I said. He isn't there."

Terry kept his eyes shut as he shuffled towards the cliff and Jack could see he didn't want to take in what might be down there. But, when he did look, even Terry couldn't deny it. Batten's body wasn't there.

His eyes were wide open now. "You're right. The guy isn't down there," he whispered. He looked out towards the horizon. " 'Ee must 'ave survived the fall and made it out to sea."

"No way," Jack said. "No one could have survived that fall and even if he had, most of his bones would have been smashed. You've got to believe me, Force Ten. He never reached the bottom of the cliff."

Terry shook his head. "I aren't stupid," he said. "If 'ee jumped, 'ee landed."

But Jack was insistent. "No. It's like I told you. There are things about Batten that you don't know. Nothing about him follows the laws of nature. None of this does. That's what's so terrifying about him. He's indestructible."

Terry still wouldn't accept it. "Nobody's indestructible, simple Jack, and 'ow come you know all this?"

Jack took him by the shoulder and turned him gently. "Come on," he said. "There's Greg and those Africans to sort out. I'll tell you on the way. But don't expect any of this to be normal."

As they climbed the hill, Jack told him everything from the déjà vu to his trips into the past – about Martha Jax and how he'd become part of her.

Terry was shaking his head at every turn in the unfolding story.

"You some kind of a medium or something?" he said, and it wasn't a question; it was more like an accusation.

"No way. It's the house and Batty Batten ... Martha Jax and Batten and me, we became like this triangle and I don't know how I got to be involved, except I happened to move into the house, and Jax and me, we're the same age ... and we've both got ginger hair."

"Do you reckon you could 'ave been 'er in another life, like reincarnation?" Terry said.

"I don't know that either," said Jack. "I don't understand any of it."

By now they were nearing the engine house, and there was an unnatural silence hanging over the place. They stopped and listened.

"Is that ghost still hoverin' up there over the Africans, scaring the wits out of them? Because there isn't no noise," Terry said.

But the ghost wasn't there and neither was the Volkswagen camper van. There was no sign of the Africans, and Greg was lying on the engine house floor, his body disturbingly motionless.

"They've killed 'im," Terry hissed and he stood there, rooted to the ground, staring, but Jack was his mother's son, and there was no way he would allow himself to make such assumptions.

He ran to the body and felt Greg's neck for a pulse. He detected one easily and Greg's body was warm. "They've just knocked him out," he said. "He'll be okay. Have you got your mobile?"

Terry nodded. "Never go nowhere without it."

"Well, phone the police, but be careful what you tell them. Say Greg's up here unconscious and tell them we need an ambulance. You can say there were a load of Africans up here too, if you like, and there was a camper van, but say the Africans and the camper van have gone. Don't tell them any more than that. It's too complicated. We can make statements later."

"Yeah, right," Terry said grimly. "If I start talkin' about ghosts and Batten takin' a leap into oblivion, they'll 'ave me certified."

Jack grinned. "You mean they haven't already?" He began running his fingers over Greg in search of broken bones and he hoped the police and the ambulance wouldn't waste any time getting there. Greg's breathing was shallow and there was a clamminess about him.

After Terry had phoned, there wasn't anything else they could do except sit and listen to the silence.

Jack's exposition of his experiences since he'd been in Tregenwyth had had an effect on Terry. He was awkward, as if all this had changed his perception and he was still struggling to come to terms with it.

Jack could understand that. For a guy with both feet rooted on terra firma, some of it wouldn't be easy to take. Being in touch with the past, moving through time portals, having this unearthly connection with a spirit; and he and Martha had conjured up what must have looked like a supernatural inferno in front of Terry with their singing.

"I'm just an ordinary guy, Force Ten," he said at last. "I'm still the simple Jack you've always known. I haven't got any unnatural powers. I'm not a time traveller or anything, not like Batten."

Terry carried on looking uncomfortably at his hands. At last, he sighed and said, "No, Jack, mate. I aren't thinkin' you're weird nor anything. It's just…I never knew all this was goin' on. I mean, whatever you say, you aren't no ordinary bloke like me, are 'ee?"

"I am," Jack said. There was a passion in his voice and he felt slightly wounded that what he'd been through had made Terry want to put him in a different place in the world. "I didn't choose for any of this to happen and I still can't come to terms with it, not properly. It was all stuck on me, and you've got to believe me, I didn't want any of it. I was happiest just being your mate down on the punt. All the other things have been driving me crazy, and none of them are going to happen again, not now that Batten's gone. I'll be a normal guy in every way from now on."

"Yeah…" Terry was still struggling. "But…"

"Look Force Ten," Jack said. He moved uncomfortably on the granite stone. "You've been my only strength since I came down here. If it wasn't for you I'd have gone mad and I don't want you thinking I'm odd. I'm just an ordinary person...and..." he swallowed. This was one of the hardest things he'd ever had to do. "I don't want you to go off being my mate just because of what's happened."

Terry looked at him and put an arm around his shoulder. "I aren't goin' to go off bein' your mate, simple Jack. It isn't that. It's just...well...after all this, I reckon I got to show you a bit more respect...besides...I aren't used to all this kind of thing – what's 'appened to you and the like. I just got to get it sorted in my head, that's all."

"That's okay, then," Jack said. "You just carry on thinking of me as the stupid guy that can't stand upright in a punt...and...I'm glad you know about it, because, in a way, that's special. You know things that have happened to me and no one else in the world knows about them."

Terry nodded. "Yeah. And we shared some of it."

"We shared the biggest bit. What's happened up here tonight is awesome."

They looked at Greg on the floor. "Do you think we should put him in the recovery position?" Jack said. "I didn't feel any broken bones."

"We could give it a go," said Terry, but as they knelt down to ease his body over, they heard the drone of a helicopter. Terry looked up. "That'll be from Culdrose. We might as well wait now until the paramedics get 'ere."

Jack took another look at Greg. His breathing was still shallow and all the time they'd been with him, he hadn't shown a glimmer of recovery. "Those African guys must have really worked him over before they left," he said. "He doesn't seem to be having any difficulty breathing though, and if he's broken something – his back or his neck, then it could do real damage moving him."

They went out onto the hill. The helicopter was swooping in over the sea, nose down like a giant mosquito, and as it neared, the power of its rotor blades shook the ground. The pilot leaned out and waved for them to move clear and they returned to the engine house, while the helicopter lowered itself onto the downs.

As soon as it landed, someone leapt out and ran across to Greg, stooping over him, examining his general state and checking for broken bones. He checked his head for fractures as well, while a couple of men emerged from the helicopter with a stretcher and as they eased the body onto its stretched canvas, Jack heard the distant sound of a police siren. He looked up to see the police Landrover bouncing across the downs, its blue light flashing.

The helicopter took Greg to Polgarthen. He was concussed and badly beaten. Jack's mum told him later that he was in intensive care for several days. When he was better, the police interviewed him.

They interviewed Jack and Terry too.

In their account, they decided to stick to the things that wouldn't stretch the police's instincts for facts and they made no reference to the paranormal. They just told them they'd heard noises under the cellar and they'd discovered a trapdoor down there. They said they'd found huge caverns beneath the cellar floor with water running in from the sea. They'd seen Batten down there with a group of African men and they thought that was suspicious. They told the police there were jetties down there and the place was done up like a subterranean harbour.

Then they said they'd noticed Batten making trips up to the cliff practically every night and they knew Greg had connections with him because, one day, they'd found him injured in Three Corners' Cove and he'd asked for Batten. Because they thought there was something odd going on, they'd followed the choirmaster up to Wheal Trennack. That's where they'd discovered him with Greg and the Africans and they'd seen a Volkswagen camper van parked by the engine house. There'd been fighting up there and raised voices, but when Batten saw them, he'd run off. He'd taken a dive over the cliff. They'd checked to see what might have happened, but when they looked over the cliff edge, they couldn't see any sign of a body down in the cove.

They went back to the mine and they'd found Greg on his own, out for the count, and the Africans and the Volkswagen camper van had gone.

The police found it hard to accept that the sight of two thirteen year old boys would make Batten jump over the cliff. They questioned them a lot about that, not only because it seemed very improbable, but because there was no body. They'd searched the whole area around Three Corners' Cove and not only was there no body in the cove, but nothing had been detected in the sea and nothing had been washed up anywhere.

They really wanted them to be sure about him jumping over, they said, because Batten was a wanted man and it looked as if he'd slipped through the net.

No matter how much they pushed, Jack couldn't tell them the whole story. He knew Batten had 'slipped through the net'. There wasn't a 'net' in the world that could have stopped him.

The police searched the cellar and the caverns with forensic teams, examining every inch of the caves, and they investigated the shaft. They said it led directly to the mine workings at Wheal Trennack.

It didn't take long to catch up with the Africans and their camper van. There weren't many roads out of Cornwall and there weren't that many bashed up Volkswagen camper vans. But when they'd apprehended them, the picture became a lot clearer.

Batten had been trafficking people from North Africa. He had a network of rich yacht owners who ferried them.

The Africans were desperate to escape the poverty and tensions of their own countries and Batten charged them outrageous prices for false passports and travel documents. The yacht owners brought them into Tregenwyth Bay at night and small dinghies ferried them through the caves into the cavern under Batten's house. But what made the crime even worse was that when Batten got them into his clutches, instead of releasing them into the country, he confiscated their false passports and papers and made them work in the Trennack mine.

He forced them to dig for minerals, tin and gold and arsenic. And then, through his network of yachts, he smuggled the ore back to Africa where the minerals were smelted and sold on the Black Market. Greg was there to keep order and the Africans hated him. That's why they were always fighting with him.

They had no way of escape because Batten had their identity papers. They were at his mercy. The camper van was used mainly by Greg to ferry food and materials for basic survival. Occasionally, when the African's had served their time, Batten would release one or two. Greg would drive them to London. It was safe. The released Africans couldn't tell anyone what was going on because they were in Britain illegally. One word to the authorities and they would have been deported back to Africa.

The police managed to round up a whole network of yacht owners and other people involved in the scheme, but the main villain was Batten, and he was never found. It puzzled the authorities, but it didn't puzzle Jack. He knew Batten for what he was, even though he couldn't tell anyone. Batten was an evil force woven like a thread into time. He'd disappeared and he would stay hidden for a century or two. Then he'd re-emerge and weave another web of corruption. Martha Jax had known that; they'd both known it and between them they'd managed to frustrate his operations. But it would need another Jack and another Martha in another age to destroy him.

After the police had finished their investigations and arrested Greg, things around the house settled into some kind of normality.

Jack's parents were contrite.

"We had no idea," his mum said. "You always maintained you didn't like that Batten fellow, and in spite of your protestations, your dad made you join his choir."

"It's a good job he did," Jack said. "Me and Terry might never have got on to him if I hadn't been in his choir."

"Was Batten the one who gave you the nightmares?" his dad asked and that irritated Jack.

It was still a 'nightmare' to him. Neither of his parents would see the truth about all this. They would never acknowledge what had really happened. "He had something to do with it, yes," he said.

There were no more instabilities in the house, but Jack was still laid low by emotions and memories.

The thought of having dealings with anyone as corrupt and as unnatural as Batten left him scarred. He had nightmares about him, and he had nightmares about Martha Jax and Barney. The nightmares about them really got to him.

Martha Jax was as much a part of him now as his own soul. She was melded into his DNA. She had shared his nerve endings, his blood, his whole being. It was as if everything about her had infiltrated him ...and that crucial, newly discovered essence of his body had been violated and murdered by Wheal Trennack over two hundred years ago. Baldwyn's men had burned her in a brushwood fire. Jack had been there. He'd been part of her as she was dying, and in the throes of death, she'd been racked by grief for her brother. Now it was as if he carried all her grief. It was seared indelibly into his psyche.

Terry noticed.

"You lost the will to live, 'ave 'ee?" he said, one Saturday afternoon.

They were watching the autumn visitors as they grabbed the last vestige of the holiday season. "It's like you aren't 'ere no more, not since we caught Batty Batten up Wheal Trennack."

"It's hard to explain," Jack said ...but ...he needed to talk to someone and Terry was the one person in the world who knew about this, the one person who'd seen Martha Jax, and Jack trusted Terry. He felt no misgivings about telling him how she had infiltrated the very substance of his existence and was part of his psyche or how it had hurt him that she'd been so violently murdered.

Terry didn't say anything, not while Jack was explaining or for a few minutes afterwards. He just sucked air through his teeth and thought. Then he said, "You remember 'er burnin' up there do 'ee? Do you know for certain that she died?"

"She didn't have a snowball's chance, Force Ten. They tied her up. And her brother was out cold, lying beside her."

"'Ave you tried finding out anything about 'er in libraries and that?"

Jack shrugged. "I've tried Googling Cornish ghosts – but I couldn't find anything about her."

"There might be somethin' local," Terry said. "Or someone 'round 'ere who knows somethin'."

Suddenly, he slid off the jetty wall.

"Where are you going?" Jack said.

"Where I'm goin', simple Jack, is where you're goin'. We're goin' up the old peoples' 'ome to do a spot of visitin'."

"Why?"

"We're goin' to see Bill Burney. 'Ee's a lovely ole boy and like I told you, 'ee lived in your 'ouse before you moved in. I know 'ee was into history – like, his ancestry – and all the other history around 'ere. There isn't nothin' that 'appened in this village for the last two hundred years Bill Burney don't know about. 'Ee might be able to tell 'ee a bit about your Martha Jax, and you'll enjoy talkin' to 'im. 'Ee's good for a gas, Bill Burney is."

22

The old peoples' home was on the hill at the back of the village.

It was a stiff climb and it left Jack breathless.

His stomach was churning because he realised he wasn't great with old people and he didn't like meeting anyone he didn't know. As for Martha Jax, he had almost moved to the phase of the 'ostrich mentality'. If there was more to find out, he wasn't convinced he wanted to know.

When they got to the home, he followed Terry into the reception hall and stood there, bristling with discomfort. One of the carers appeared. She was a middle-aged woman and she smiled at Terry, acknowledging Jack with a nod.

"Bill around is 'ee?" Terry said.

"He's in the conservatory having his cup of tea," she said.

"Do 'ee think 'ee'd 'ave time for a chat?" said Terry.

The woman laughed. "Can a duck? I'll tell him he's got a couple of visitors. Just hang on there a minute."

Jack looked around uncertainly. The entrance was very much like a hotel foyer. "Will it be all right talking to him?" he said. "He doesn't know me."

Terry laughed. "You're a weird bloke, simple Jack. You take on ghosts and Batty Batten without blinkin', and you're scared witless at the thought of meetin' an old man who wouldn't hurt a fly."

"Yeah, but I'm not into old people," Jack said.

"You'll like Bill Burney and if it'll make you 'appier, I'll do the talkin'."

The carer came back. She was still smiling. "His lordship is receiving guests," she said. "You know the way, Terry, boy. Who's your friend?"

"Jack O'Hagan," Terry said. "'Ee've moved into Bill's old place."

The carer raised an eyebrow and smiled again. "Plenty to talk about, then," she said.

Jack followed Terry down some carpeted corridors into the conservatory. Bill Burney was sitting in a garden chair, balancing a cup and saucer on his knee. He was a lean looking guy and his arthritic hands gripping the cup were corrugated with blue-ribbed veins. He had a long face, bristling with white stubble and there were thin horn-rimmed glasses resting on his beak of a nose. He was wearing a cap and he smiled when he saw Terry.

"How 'ee doin', Bill?" Terry said, grabbing a chair.

"Mustn't grumble, boy. Just 'avin my afternoon's. If you want a cup of tea, ask Evelyn there. She'll bring 'ee a cup and a few biscuits too, shouldn't wonder." He pressed a talisman-like disc hanging from his neck and chuckled. "Only meant to use this in emergencies, but she don't mind."

The carer looked through the door and she was laughing. "One of these days, Bill Burney, I'm taking that thing away from you. What is it now?"

"Think you can rustle up a cup of tea and a biscuit for these boys, do 'ee?" Bill said.

She nodded. "I'll see what I can do, as it's you. Wouldn't do it for everybody, mind."

Bill looked across at Jack. "Grab a chair, boy. Make yourself at home."

"This is Jack O'Hagan, Bill," Terry said. "'Ee've moved into your old place."

Bill's eyes lit up. "'Ave 'ee?" he said. "Lovely old 'ouse that is. Like it up there, do 'ee?"

"He's interested in the history of it, Bill," Terry said. "We think there was smugglin' goin' on there, one time."

Jack dragged a chair across from the wall and settled beside Terry. "We found this cavern under the cellar," he said.

Bill nodded. "Yes, there are caves down there and there were big smuggling operations going on when a man called Trelawny lived there towards the end of the eighteenth century. That 'ouse was a centre for smuggling in Tregenwyth. Trelawny and Squire Polglaise, the one that owned Polgaise's Bank in Polgarthen and a man called Baldwyn, the magistrate, they were all in it up to their necks and they did all their operation from that 'ouse."

Jack's eyes widened. He hadn't remembered about Polglaise, but as soon as Bill mentioned him, he knew. There *was* a man called Polglaise… and the bank… Jax put money in that bank.

"I've been finding out one or two things since we moved in," Jack said. "I knew about Trelawny and the Baldwyn guy."

"You done well to find that out," said Bill. "You only been in there for a month or two. And Baldwyn, 'ee was a nasty piece of work by all accounts. They did a raid on the house, you know, caught them red handed with the brandy stacked in the caverns, but Baldwyn disappeared. They never found 'im."

Suddenly, there was a rush of adrenaline in Jack. It was as if Bill was opening the gates to things that he already knew, only, where the jigsaw was still in pieces for him, Bill had it already assembled, and that was amazing.

"Was there a servant girl?" Jack asked.

Bill looked slightly taken aback. "You know about she?" he said. "You 'ave done your homework, boy."

"Martha Jax?" Jack said, and his heart was thumping.

But the fact that he knew Martha Jax by name seemed to have an odd effect on Bill. He breathed in sharply and looked at Terry. His voice was shaking when he spoke. "'Ee knows about Martha, boy. That's… I don't know. 'Ee've found out about Martha."

His reaction wasn't what Jack had expected. He didn't want to upset the old boy.

"Is that special, Bill?" Terry said and immediately Jack said:

"We needn't talk about it if it upsets you, Mr Burney."

"It's all right, boy," Bill said, although he looked quite emotional and his hands were trembling around his cup. And yet there seemed to be a glimmer of a smile. "You got no idea what this do mean to me," he said. Then he added something that rocked Jack to his heels. "Martha Jax, you see, she was my great, great grandmother – well, more greats than I could count really, but she was my great, grandmother."

Jack's mouth opened, but he couldn't speak. The implications of what Bill had just said were so massive that, for a moment, he could hardly think straight. But he did manage to blurt out, "But she was burnt to death up by Wheal Trennack." His mind was reeling out of control.

"You know about that too?" Bill said. He looked almost as shocked as Jack. "It took me years of digging in books and looking up records to find all that out. You done really well, my son."

"But…" The contradictions in Jack's head were muddying every thought that struggled to the surface. "But how? If she died up on those downs, how come she had children?"

"She didn't die up there, boy," Bill said. "Her brother, Barney Jax, he was up there too, see?"

"But he was unconscious," Jack said.

Bill looked at Terry again, still totally bewildered. "'Ow do this boy know so much?" he said.

Terry was grinning. "You just tell us your story, Bill. We'll tell you about Jack later."

"Barney revived, boy," Bill said. "He saw Martha bound up there beside him and 'ee cut her free. They escaped. They got back to Polgarthen and the customs men did another raid. They retook the brandy and carted it off to the excise headquarters in Gweek. Barney was a young dragoon, you see?"

Jack knew about that, but hearing what Bill said was churning his stomach. It was turning everything he knew upside down.

"Martha went back to her mother," Bill said. "Her mother was a widow come down from Devon. Later Martha married a local farmer – Thomas Burney, and I'm their direct descendant."

It was then that Evelyn brought in the tea and Jack sat there balancing his cup and biscuit – and there were so many questions he wanted to ask. To know that Martha Jax' life had not been torn away in her prime up on those cliffs, to know that she'd gone on to live a full life – it was as if a dark cloud had been lifted from him and for the first time since he'd set foot in Tregenwyth, he felt at peace – completely and utterly without a care. His soul-host in the eighteenth century had survived and no brutal violation of the Tregenwyth men had snatched her life away ... and to be in a room with someone whose very DNA had come from Martha Jax' genes – someone who would have traits of her personality woven into his bones, someone who was an extension of her soul – whose flesh was her flesh – that was something else. Somehow, Jack was seeing Bill Burney in a way that he couldn't begin to fathom.

"I found out all this years ago," Bill was saying. "Long before there was these fangled computers like there is nowadays. All you got to do now, so they tell me, is press a few buttons and it's all done for you. I knew Martha Jax was servant girl to Trelawny and I knew she lived in that 'ouse where you're livin' now, boy. That's why I bought the place. It was like my ancestral home if you like. But I still don't understand 'ow you've found out so much. Did you do it on a computer? And… to know she was up on they cliffs when they set fire to everything – I didn't know you could find that sort of thing on a computer."

"How Jack knows – it's a long story, Bill," Terry said. "And it'll make the hairs stand up on your 'ead."

Bill laughed and shook his gnarled fist at Terry. "I 'aven't got no hairs on my head to stand up as you well know, Terry Blewett. That's why I do wear this cap, to keep my head warm. You're a cheeky little blighter."

Terry chuckled. "It's an awesome story though, and we'll tell you if you like. You don't mind, do 'ee, simple

Jack? Tellin' Bill Burney what's 'appened to you since you been livin' in 'is 'ouse?"

Jack swallowed. He wanted to tell him everything. He didn't quite know how to gauge his feelings for Bill. Martha Jax had been Jack's soul partner. In another age, in some indescribable way, he'd been part of her and she'd been part of him. And now, he was in the presence of her flesh and blood in the form of this old man. That was something so special; it was almost as if he was in her presence. "I'll do my best," he said, and they told Bill the whole story.

He seemed to understand, and his soft eyes looking back at Jack, made him feel the bond between himself and Martha even more strongly. "It's like you raised my grandmother from her grave, boy," Bill said. "And you was in her head, re-living all her feelings and experiences. And to think she chose you to share her life with. It's like a miracle. I knowed there were tales of her haunting Trelawny's Wood... but... you walked with her through they woods."

Jack had never known feelings like it in his life. "And the fact that you're related to her, makes you a very special guy to me, Mr Burney," he said.

Bill gave him a broad smile. "Call me Bill, boy," he said. "Everybody does, and come 'ere and shake an old man's hand."

They spent the next hour chatting and Bill was so full of knowledge about the house, about Martha Jax, about the smuggling. He seemed to know everything there was to know about Tregenwyth and for Jack, every moment of that hour was precious. "He's an amazing guy," he said as they made their way back down the hill.

"I told you you'd like 'im," Terry said. "We must go and see 'im again sometime."

"Any time you like."

They didn't say a lot more. Jack had a whole new world to think about, and the contentment inside him made the afternoon glow with warmth.

They went out in the punt, and afterwards, at Jack's instigation, Terry took a couple of mackerel up to the old peoples' home to see if they'd fry them for Bill's supper.

Meanwhile, Jack headed for home… and… for the first time in his life, he was looking forward to getting through that door. He wanted to be in the house where Martha Jax had lived and where they'd shared the battle with Batten. Now that he knew she hadn't died a brutal death at Wheal Trennack, and now that he knew Bill Burney, it was as if the house had changed its status – as if it was his ancestral home as well. He was excited at the thought of being there.

But he had bargained without his parents.

As he shoved through to the kitchen, swinging a string of mackerel over his shoulder, he was caught in mid-step. One glance at his mum and dad told him something wasn't right.

They were both sitting at the table with pained, determined looks on their faces and Dad got up, putting an arm around Jack's waist and giving it a gentle squeeze.

"Someone dead, is there?" Jack said, but his dad was already in full flood.

"Jack, old boy," he was saying. "Your mum and I, we've been doing some serious thinking."

"You don't want to do too much of that at your age," he said. He wasn't in the mood for all this.

"Don't be flippant, Jack," Mum snapped, and his dad ploughed on.

"We haven't been blind to your situation here, what with that Batten fellow living next door and those things you and your mate uncovered."

"He's called Terry Blewett. I keep telling you, Dad. Give the guy a name."

Dad began to show signs of irritation. "Look Jack, we've been doing some real soul searching here and it's important. We've decided that it isn't fair on you, making you live here after all you've been through. We can see the place makes you unhappy, so, your mum and I, we've decided to put the house on the market… look for somewhere else away from all this, somewhere in Polgarthen perhaps. What do you say?"

Jack tore himself away and stared at his father. He couldn't believe what he'd just heard.

They were going to sell Bill Burney's place and he'd only just discovered the truth about it.

He looked around the kitchen, and in his mind, he could see the glimmering candle light of Jax' midnight toils. He saw her in her white cowl by an oak dresser. He heard the ticking of a long-cased clock in the passage. There were horses' hooves on cobbles, and as these images infiltrated his head, he warmed to every one of them.

"You'd better not put it on the market," he said. "I love this place, Dad. It's a part of me. Its history is bound up inside me. No way are you going to sell it, not now or ever."

His dad's eyebrows shot up and he looked totally lost for words. It was becoming a habit with him, Jack thought. Even his mum looked taken aback. "History bound up inside you?" she snapped. "Whatever happened to 'It's a dump, a rickety, musty old rat hole.'?"

Jack grinned. "Well, Dad's been doing a bit of redecorating, hasn't he? And anyway, are you sure I said that?"

"You certainly did," Mum said. "And ever since you've been here, you've been like someone displaced – those fits – and the moods. Frankly, Jack, we were afraid you were going out of your mind sometimes."

He shrugged and headed for the sink. There was no way he was taking time to explain all that again.

"Look," he said, picking up the potato peeler. "I can't tell you how, but, something's changed, and now, it's like … I love this old house." He turned around and laughed at the dumbfounded expressions on his parents' faces. "I tell you what," he said. "I'll make a deal, right? You forget about selling the house and I'll give Dad a hand with the dinner. We can have *pomme de terre au gratin* with the fried mackerel, how would that be?"

Dad stared. "I don't know, Jack," he said. "Sometimes you're a real enigma, but if you really want to stay, we're delighted. I'm glad you can sense the history and atmosphere of the place at last. We've always felt it, and we don't really want to sell. It was all for you."

Jack grinned. A sense of history and atmosphere? His dad and his mum hadn't the first idea. They hadn't sensed any of the history or the atmosphere. They hadn't even been aware that any history had been going on.

The secrets of this old place were not his parents'. They belonged to him and to Martha Jax and to old Bill Burney up on the hill. The house would never be special for anyone else, not like it was for them. And as far as he was concerned, he would be happy to live here for the rest of his life.

Lightning Source UK Ltd.
Milton Keynes UK
UKOW01f2328050516

273633UK00001B/1/P